On Christmas Day, 1910, Elinor Grace, traveller, scholar and
archaeologist, left Aden clandestinely for the Red Sea port of
Hodeidah. Her goal was to uncover the truth about the Queen
of Sheba's legendary capital at Mareb on the fringes of
Arabia's Empty-Quarter. But as she set sail from Aden she
wondered why she had agreed to travel with the irascible
Scot, James Fergusson. What were Fergusson's true
intentions? For a naturalist he had an uncommonly poor eye
for wildlife. Why was he so intent on their joining forces, and
why had she said yes when she was used to travelling alone?

The expedition was ill-fated from the start. Opinion has it that
Elinor never reached her goal and that the expedition ended
in failure. Jennifer Potter's inspired story tells otherwise. The
intrigue that has been erased from official files unnervingly
unfolds as Elinor journeys into depravity and betrayal and
into the dark quarters of the heart.

THE LONG LOST JOURNEY

FOR CHRISTOPHER

THE LONG LOST JOURNEY

JENNIFER POTTER

BLOOMSBURY

First published in Great Britain 1989

Copyright © 1989 by Jennifer Potter

This paperback edition published 1991

The moral right of the author has been asserted

Bloomsbury Publishing Ltd, 2 Soho Square, London W1V 5DE

A CIP catalogue record for this book
is available from the British Library

ISBN 0 7475 0713 9

Printed in Great Britain by Richard Clay plc, Suffolk

CONTENTS

ACKNOWLEDGEMENTS

In fitting together the pieces of Elinor Grace's lost journey to Māreb, some eighty years after the event, I am indebted to the India Office Library and Records and most especially the letters, memoranda and telegrams of His Majesty's Vice-Consul at Hodeidah on which I have drawn heavily. An abridged version of one of his letters appears on p. 107 by kind permission of the Controller of Her Majesty's Stationery Office. Its Crown copyright is acknowledged, as is that of the first epigraph.[1]

Other sources have provided valuable information and inspiration. These include: Admiralty: Naval Intelligence Division, *A Handbook of Arabia, Vol. 1, General*, ID 1128, HMSO, 1920, and *Western Arabia and the Red Sea, BR 527 (Restricted)*, June 1946; G. W. Bury, *Arabia Felix or the Turks in Yamen*, Macmillan and Co. Ltd, 1915; W. B. Harris, *A Journey through the Yemen and Some General Remarks on that Country*, William Blackwood and Sons, 1893; W. Phillips, *Qataban and Sheba: Exploring Ancient Kingdoms on the Biblical Spice Routes of Arabia*, Victor Gollancz Ltd, 1955; H. St John Philby, *The Queen of Sheba*, Quartet Books Ltd, 1981; and A. J. B. Wavell, *A Modern Pilgrim in Mecca and a Siege in Sanaa*, Constable and Co. Ltd, 1912.

The spelling of proper names follows the system of transliteration adopted for *A Handbook of Arabia* (HMSO, 1920), and set out on pps 612 to 618 of that publication.

The first biblical account of the Queen of Sheba's journey to Solomon appears in 1 Kings 10:1–13. It is reproduced almost exactly in 2 Chronicles 9:1–12; and fleeting references occur in the New Testament, Matthew 12:42 and Luke 11:31. Relevant passages in the *Qur'ān* may be found in Chapters 27 ('The Ant') and 34 ('Sheba'). The drawings appearing in the text are taken from Carsten Niebuhr, *Voyage en Arabie et en d'autres Pays circonvoisins, Vol I*, S. J. Baalde, Amsterdam and J. van Schoohoven and Company, Utrecht, 1776.

Finally, my special thanks to Richard Rayner for his enthusiasm, Lucretia Stewart for her acumen and Ianthe Maclagan for her patient advice. All faults remaining are entirely my own.

1. IOLR references: R/20/A/1523 and L/P&S/10/259

It should, however, be understood that HMG do not desire to encourage the exploration of Arabia.
– The Most Honourable The Marquis of Crewe KG, His Majesty's Secretary of State for India, to the Government of India, Foreign Department (Secret, External), 8 November 1912

Beyond the fountain the road was empty, and though I knew it well I was struck again by the incredible desolation of it. No life, no flowers, the bare stalks of last year's thistles, the bare hills and the stony road.
– Gertrude Bell, *The Desert and the Sown*

PART ONE

FROM THE RED SEA TO SHEHĀRAH

25 December 1910

Aden's fetters shaken off at last, I begin my journal in good heart this Christmas Day, 1910, having dined like a queen on boiled sheep's brains and a plum pudding raided from my stores. Beyond my cabin rolls the sea's dark swell, spangled with phosphorescence, and my spirit darts about expectantly, leap-frogging all manner of tribulations and the rigours of the journey to come.

I do so love beginnings, when all is possible. The siren sounds of the sea draw me onwards and I listen entranced to the incantatory tales of the ship's mate, a native Somali, who clusters with his fellows near my door. Though I may long for Maunton, and all the quiet comforts of home, I know that my place is here, out in the world, and that I cross these empty wastes even in dreams.

My dear sister Jane will never understand how I feel. She quizzes me about where I have been and what I have done and where I shall journey to next; and between us, when we talk of such things, stretches a gulf far wider than that between Africa and Arabia. And so she smiles sweetly and stays at home, thinking me uncannily odd for my boldness.

To keep them in my thoughts, I opened my presents as soon as we had passed the rocky promontory of Ras 'Imrān and left the lights of Aden far behind. Mother's shawl will prove a godsend in the mountains: its strong Persian blues enliven my rather ordinary plainness, making me feel quite handsome, if that were possible. Not handsome like Jane, who shines in every firmament, but handsome enough for present company. As for Father's books, he always knows what I want. I had to busy myself at once to stop feeling sad.

The hours lengthen as we drift towards dawn. I cannot breathe, much less sleep. Another day, another night at anchor off Hodeidah, God willing, in this kettle of a mailship (we cannot land after dusk), waiting for the morrow when my real journey begins.

A moment ago the story-teller stopped abruptly on a rising note, his tale left hanging in the air. Perhaps he was disturbed, or lost his audience to sleep. I may now take a walk on deck, stepping over the sleeping forms of the poorer passengers, catching the breeze where I can and hoping I might encounter Mr Fergusson, awake.

26 December 1910

I fear I shall go mad with boredom. Here we are, drifting about the Red Sea, having rounded the Bāb el-Mandeb at a fine speed and passed the island of Perim at first light, a tawny blot that shifted in the incandescent seas. Now the skies have turned grey, the coastline has disappeared and the engines have broken down.

The Captain says we are somewhere to the south of Mocha. 'Somewhere?' I asked crossly. 'You can't be more precise than that?' He laughed and offered to show me his stamp collection. The Chief Engineer, I'm told, is doing all he can, which to judge by the half-hearted bangings and clatterings from the bowels of the ship is not very much. I fail to understand why people with a mechanical bent cannot take better care of their engines. I never let my camels break down so inconveniently, just when we are on the point of getting somewhere.

My fellow passengers take it all in their stride. Dr Ahmed, a penguin of a man connected to some public works in Jiddah, has settled himself in a deck chair, my deck chair, and now reads aloud to himself from a newspaper. Three Turkish officers, bound, like myself, for Hodeidah, are ensconced under an awning to play cards somewhat raucously. They look a slovenly bunch in ill-fitting uniforms and decidedly drooping moustaches. Inuring oneself to misfortune is all very well, but this sort of slack fatalism allows the centre to fall apart. One cannot win wars unless one is dressed for the part.

Mr Fergusson, I see, has again walked the length of the deck to inspect his boxes which are lashed untidily to the hatches. The Captain said they were far too heavy to lower into the hold for such a short journey; I wonder what he keeps in them.

Last night, when I surfaced for air, I found him camped on the top smoking a pipe. Close to, a ship's beacon blinked on and off, consigning him every few seconds to Arabia's dark night. Thinking he had not seen me, it gave me a thrill to watch him unobserved.

He turned when least expected – my step was light, he can't have heard my approach – and stared at me hard as if he tried to fit a purpose to my person, and a name, though we are sworn companions with a common goal. On the point of re-introducing myself, his puzzled frown gave way to a more relaxed air.

'Ah, there you are, Miss Grace,' he said in that soft Scottish burr of his. 'You can't sleep, I suppose. Neither can I. All this journeying . . . Makes my gut ache.'

'Then why travel, sir?'

The light caught his face. A wicked amusement glinted in his eyes. 'Don't you feel it?' he said, sweeping his hand across the black hole of night. 'There's a world out there waiting for us. A whole ripe world, ready for the plucking.'

'Well, yes, I suppose there is. There's certainly much to be done. Your business for the British Museum . . .'

'Hang the British Museum. Just look, won't you.

There . . . ' He jabbed a finger at the stars. 'And there . . . It's ours, Miss Grace, ours for the taking.'

I clutched at the coat-tails of his enthusiasm and felt myself swept off my feet. Mr Fergusson is that sort of man. Tall, erect, with black Celtic brows, he speaks with the fervour of a Scottish pastor of the hell-fire variety. But there's a wildness to him that hints at Romany and darker secrets between the sheets, giving him altogether a changeling's air.

'The purpose of your journey, sir,' I ventured shyly. 'I mean, you are a naturalist, I take it. You said . . . '

'Of course I'm a naturalist. Aren't we all? I've certain business to conclude.'

'There's a war brewing. The General at Aden told me so himself. If you've business in mind, it's not very wise.'

'Wise, Miss Grace? Why should we be wise? We'll show them what we're made of, you and I.'

'I'd like that, sir. I mean . . . '

He looked up sharply. 'What was that?'

I heard the faint chugging of the ship's engines, nothing more. But, as I moved to reassure him, a shadow fell between us on deck; the Captain's, I think.

Mr Fergusson saw it too. He ducked his head and said quickly, 'We were agreed. We shouldn't know each other yet. Please go at once, before it's too late.'

I did as I was bid, of course, and after a turn on deck retired to my cabin, a little hurt that he should stick to his games beyond their natural life. In Aden, such subterfuges were necessary to give slip to the General, who must not know where I am headed. But here, where no one knows me from Eve . . . I can't imagine why I agreed to travel with him, I who am accustomed to travelling alone. Good sense tells me to break off our agreement, and yet I find myself strangely drawn to his intemperate moods, his bold black looks, and best of all I like his brimstony eyes.

It's no good. I must put him out of my thoughts and find

some other means to occupy myself while we drift helplessly through the doldrums to the accompaniment of the engineer's clatterings. But what can I do? I've read Mr Mills's notes until his figures dance inside my brain. He's asked for daily readings of the barometer and of the wet and dry bulb thermometers, as this corner of Arabia is a blank page as far as accurate meteorological observations are concerned. I cannot read. I cannot talk to Mr Fergusson. I have positively no desire to view Captain Pearson's stamp collection. I shall not play cards with Turkish *canaille*. As for Dr Ahmed, he's far too busy talking to himself to pay much heed to me. I could always engage in correspondence, but fear that my lowness of spirits would dispirit those I seek to please. I wish this waiting time were past. I've had enough of shilly-shallying in millpond seas.

Please God, the engines have kicked into life. If we reach Hodeidah by morning I shall reward the Chief Engineer with a sovereign, and recant the worst of my words.

27 *December 1910*

My journey has begun. I've stood on the sands of Arabia, smelt the heavy salt winds blowing in from the south-west, made the acquaintance of Dr George Wendell, HBM's Vice-Consul at Hodeidah, his wife and daughter too, and found myself temporary lodgings on the sea front. At least I'm spared the horrors of the casino, as the wretched caravanserai is called (I trust ironically), a miserable two-storey building stuffed to the brim with Turkish soldiers of the lowest sort, all shouting and spitting on the floor. I would not wish my dogs to breathe its fly-blown air. But Wendell came smartly to my aid: he seems endearingly practical and quite willing to lend a hand.

We reached Hodeidah shortly before sunrise and anchored some three miles from the shore. I was already on deck. The

Turkish soldiers lay slumped under their awning. To judge from the empty wine flasks scattered about their chairs they had made a fine night of it. Two of the fellows snored in counterpoint, the third had passed out completely.

For such moments as these do I undertake my journeys. The wind had dropped, the sea was flat as glass, and in the distance the whitewashed houses of Hodeidah and shaky minarets dissolved into the shimmering sky. As I watched, the town moved, I swear it, shifted to the left, hovered, a mirage trick, of course. I don't mean the buildings upped and walked, but I felt deeply thrilled, as if I were about to step from the ordinary world of the Khedivial steamship into the territory of dreams. Had I not, in my mind's eye, Manzoni's sketch of Hodeidah and the mountains behind, clear-edged, complete, I would have seen no gaunt jagged hills, no central highlands, nothing between the shoreline and the sky.

I looked for Mr Fergusson, wishing to share this moment with him, even in silence if he persisted in his unreasonable demands. Thinking he must have slept the night among his baggage, I walked towards the stern where a second sleight of hand awaited me. The boxes had gone. All that remained were some ropes, a smear of oil, a scrap of paper caught among the coils. I picked it up, curious. It bore roughly one half of an address in Jibuti. What did it mean? I asked myself. He can't, surely, have jettisoned his boxes out to sea?

Captain Pearson found me pondering the problem, and enquired if I had breakfasted. Thanking him kindly, I said my hunger could wait.

'It'll be some time before you're done. You'll take something before you leave my ship.' He sent a steward for coffee and a plate of stale Egyptian buns, a kindness gruffly performed, and yet I like a man who issues commands. He was anyway right: by the time we had embarked in the sanbūq with our equipment, disembarked at the other end and engineered our passage through customs it was long past midday.

I have to report that Mr Fergusson was not of our company. When questioned, the Captain revealed that he had changed his mind and would now stay with the ship as far as Musaw-wa‘, or maybe Suākin: Mr Fergusson, it seems, is rather vague about his movements. In anticipation of reported storms north of Hodeidah, his boxes had been stored below in the hold.

'Where is he now?' I asked, alarm breaking in my voice.

'Where the devil takes the man.' The Captain's manner cautioned me. I should not press him further and yet I guessed he was more rattled than he cared to admit.

The news disturbed me greatly. Mr Fergusson is a strange fish; I can't think what he means. First he accosts me in the *sūqs* of Aden – a total stranger – suggesting casually that we should travel together into el-Yemen, a country to which he had heard I was destined. (Aden is a most peculiar town. Others know one's thoughts before one has thought them oneself.) Then, on the point of arrival, he disappears in a puff of smoke. Although his behaviour calls into question his reliability – and it's as well to know these things before one sets out for the wilds – I felt his loss keenly and anyway believe that partings should be properly done.

Putting a brave face on his last-minute desertion, I climbed into the *sanbūq*, determined to cast the whole episode firmly from mind. These things are better done alone. But my fellow travellers did little to improve my temper. In addition to the Turkish officers, unwashed and smelling sourly of sharp wine, our party consisted of a fat Greek who had once or twice on board ship attempted to press-gang me into conversation; and a German count, or so he claimed, who clambered down the makeshift ladder at the last possible moment and plopped himself beside me, grinning furtively like a bank clerk who has just embezzled the reserves.

As we neared the shore, my spirits failed to revive. The tall houses and minarets of Hodeidah, so picturesque from a distance, have fallen into an advanced state of dilapidation for which I hold the Turks responsible. One cannot conceive of a race more lacking in that quality of foresight which has made our Empire great. The harbour, built only lately, hasn't the draught for loaded boats and I was carried to shore on the shoulders of a Negro stevedore who couldn't decide whether to drape my skirts round his neck or let them trail in the waves. In the end he did both and dropped me roughly on the strand along with my stores.

At the Turkish Customs House I was rudely questioned about the authenticity of my visa from the Ottoman Embassy in London and, out of spite, forced to open each one of my stores.

When the comedy had run its course I sent a boy to seek out the Vice-Consul who was run to earth in the open *sūq* to the north of the town, where he had been called to the aid of a British Indian merchant involved in some unpleasant wrangle over hides. He sent his *kavass* to take me to the Consulate, a ramshackle building across from the plage. Its wooden lattice window looked ready to drop off at the next sea breeze and crash to the ground below. I side-stepped the entrance, and was taken up to the first floor where I was welcomed by the lady of the house, Mrs Mary Wendell, and her young daughter, whom I had disturbed at their lessons.

I warmed to her at once. If one must serve one's time in such a miserable outpost as Hodeidah, she'd make a first-rate companion. She seems, above all, sensible, and accepted my arrival in her tidy house as an everyday occurrence, though she must yearn for company. She asked about my plans. When I explained that I hoped to visit the ruins at Māreb, on the other side of the mountains, she said, 'You'll have to disguise yourself a little. They're not very partial to foreigners, over there. Show Miss Grace your schoolbook, Lizzie dear.'

The child, a sandy-haired sprig of about eight, passed me a large notebook filled with dislocated phrases. I marvelled at the dramas they concealed: 'The hills are green today. The boy Husein sometimes plays cricket instead of going to the mosque with his uncles. Can you show me the way to Piccadilly? Mrs Tibbs often does the cleaning.'

'Have you been to England?' I asked the girl, who glanced shyly towards her mother then shook her head.

'Elizabeth was born in India,' intervened Mrs Wendell. 'In Lucknow. My husband's a serving Army officer, you know. In the medical corps.'

'So it's Dr Wendell, is it?' I'm sure at Aden they speak of him as plain Mr Wendell.'

'My husband doesn't worry too much about things like that.'

After a short silence, she said abruptly, 'They pay him a pittance, you know: £370 a year. For that, they expect him to write his own reports, which he does at night. And, when it all gets too much, he hires a temporary clerk whom he pays out of his own pocket.'

She kissed her daughter then looked at me brightly. 'Do you have influence?' she asked. The question startled me in its directness. We had only just met and here she was enlisting my aid.

The light in her eyes was snuffed as quickly as it had come. 'I don't expect you do. My husband's served them well for twelve years. A service, I might add, rendered cheerfully and unostentatiously in the most trying conditions. What thanks does he get for his pains? None whatsoever, Miss Grace. They won't even pay his passage home.'

With that she pushed the conversation aside and talked to the child about geometry. I'll put in a good word for him if I can. Marooned as he is amidst the scorching sun and life-draining climate of the Red Sea littoral, a place of pestilence and malarial fevers playing host to an unruly garrison of Turks, his only society (apart from a wife and child) provided by Indian merchants and a smattering of Greeks, he should at least be properly compensated.

———

The good doctor himself arrived shortly afterwards and I was able to observe their deep regard for one another. He has the bristling alertness of an Airedale terrier crossed with the dogged enthusiasm of a spaniel, and if the resultant brew looks slightly peculiar – he has short sandy hair and big ears – he has a mongrel's plainer good sense.

Once introduced, he settled himself in an armchair, the child on his knee, and asked a few pertinent questions to satisfy himself that I needed no introduction to the ways of the Turk. On this, I put his mind at rest. Among other things I carry a letter to the Vali, Mohammed 'Ali Pasha, whom I met once in Syria. Wendell looked impressed at my connections.

'As long as one lets it be known,' I said, 'that one comes of a good family and has the support of one's Government and King, one comes to no harm.'

'So the General at Aden . . . He gave you his blessing, I take it, for this journey of yours?'

'Not exactly . . . In fact, he really wasn't too enamoured of the idea. The present troubles, you understand. He went so far as to suggest I tried my hand at Morocco. Heaven knows why. It boasts of precious few antiquities and what few sights there are have mostly been explored already.'

'Didn't think he would. We're not supposed to encourage travellers.'

'Nonsense. General Sir John Harris is a very dear friend.'

'Damned awkward, from his point of view.'

'I'm sure the General had nothing to do with it. I simply refused to oil every grasping palm thrust my way. You know what they're like in Aden. I tried to get a boat to take me east to Makalla, but Cowasjee Dinshaw & Bros dragged their heels then claimed an outbreak of smallpox in the Protectorate. Strange that no one else had heard of it. All boats west, they said, were fully booked for months.'

'Cowasjee Dinshaw, you say? They never sneeze unless the General's caught a cold. You could have tried overland.'

'I did. No one would hire me the necessary camels, except one wily rogue who swore he had some waiting at Lahej. I didn't trust his face and his price was ridiculous.'

'You got here anyway,' said Dr Wendell, flapping his ears like a spaniel who basks in his master's approbation. 'I say, are you quite all right?'

He must have noticed my sudden silence. I didn't explain that my success in obtaining passage was entirely due to a third party. Without Mr Fergusson, I'd still be trailing round the sights of Aden.

Dr Wendell looked worried. Perhaps he thought I was about to faint. 'I'll have to tell him, you know,' he went on gently. 'The General, I mean.'

'Is that really necessary? He'll be frightfully cross. They think I've gone home. Captain Kincaid, his ADC, waved me goodbye.'

'Nice chap, Kincaid. Don't let's worry about that, my dear. The General will have to know, I'm afraid. This is India's patch, after all. But I know what I'll do. I'll send him a letter through the Turkish post. He's always complaining about the cost of my telegrams. You'll be long gone before the General hears about this.'

That settled, luncheon was announced. Dr Wendell had wanted to set out immediately to procure for me some lodgings but his wife remonstrated most sensibly. One must not walk these sun-baked streets on an empty stomach. Their cook, a Goanese, provided an acceptable table and we talked of the current unrest in the *vilayet*.

Dr Wendell paid me the compliment of telling me the worst, so that I might prepare accordingly. Since his return a week ago from Kamarān Island at the end of the pilgrim season, the bazaars have seethed with rumours that an uprising will take place shortly in the mountains. Armed bands have appeared around the capital, San'ā, and most of the Arabs have buried their tribal hatchets and flocked to the standard of Imam

Yahya, spiritual leader of at least some of the highland tribes. They'll soon fall out again, I'm sure, but in the mean time Dr Wendell believes that, as long as I carry decent arms (he recommends the .30 Winchester or a Savage), hire myself a first-class servant, and keep my head out of the cross-fire, I shall come to no harm. The Turks and the rebels will be far too busy playing catch-as-catch-can in the mountains to pay much attention to me.

Although in Aden they laugh at Wendell as a Jeremiah, he treats the rumoured revolt with all the consequence of a shooting party, at which he plainly anticipates much sport. Curious, I asked why he was willing to shoulder on my account the General's wrath. He turned very solemn and called his masters fools. By closing the gate to British explorations, they had opened the field to every harebrained foreigner wishing to leave his footprints in the sands.

'Hear, hear,' said Mrs Wendell.

I felt quite touched by their sentiments.

Dr Wendell went out directly after luncheon and in no time returned, having rented on my behalf a house on the water-front. The ground floor is used as a granary, the floor above it empty save for the rats whose scratchings I hear even now, but my chambers are cleaner than I could rightfully expect. It has a funny wattle hut on the roof where I may seek the cool air at night.

Tomorrow, Dr Wendell says I must present myself to the Commissaire, the officer in charge of police, and will be summoned to attend on the Mutessarif, or Governor, Mahir Bey, by all accounts a very bad man. From now I'll have little time for writing. There is so much to be done.

29 December 1910

My preparations progress apace. First, I've been fortunate in that vexatious business of servants, finding myself on Dr

Wendell's recommendation one of the butcher caste from the maritime hills. His name is Yūsuf. He wears a white skirt or kilt, a black turban sprigged with basil, and a sleeveless black coat. He chews *kat*, of course, but his addiction is kept within bounds. Having served for a time as a mess boy in Aden he carries a testimonial that declares he's neither more nor less honest than other servants but enjoys one particular advantage: he knows how to boil a guinea fowl. I hired him on the spot. With his broad Abyssinian nose and straggly pigtails he looks like a music hall genie, and speaks the most atrocious English I ever wish to hear.

I've also paid my courtesy calls on the Turks. The Commissaire received me politely enough and after we had stalked each other round interminable bushes, he asked about my plans. I explained that with permission from his Embassy in London and the support of HMG (moral, I hastened to add, not financial) I intended to mount an expedition to Māreb on the western edges of the Ruba' el-Khāli.

The Commissaire raised one eyebrow. 'What does your Government expect in return?'

'My motives are purely historical, sir. I'm a scholar by profession, and archaeologist. Since Glaser's extraordinary journey to Māreb over twenty years ago, many questions hang in the air, not least the ruins' much-vaunted connection with Sheba.'

He shifted uneasily in his seat.

'The Queen of Sheba,' I said. 'Saba, you call it. In the *Qur'ān*. You must remember. She visits King Solomon in Jerusalem. We've much the same tale in the Bible, without your more imaginative touches. Talking hoopoe birds and the like . . .'

'I don't quite see . . .'

'Of course you don't. That's not the point. In the New Testament she's called the Queen of the South, which is ridiculous, I'm certain of it. She never came from here at all.'

Noting the Commissaire's increasing bewilderment, I went on more quickly, 'Whoever wrote Matthew's Gospel got his dates muddled up. Saba refers to a tribe, you see, not a place. In Solomon's time, the tribe of Saba still roamed the north. It didn't migrate southwards until much later: my guess is towards the middle of the seventh century BC, by which time Solomon had been dead 300 years. If I can examine the ruins myself . . . '

'Not possible,' he said glumly and turned his back on me.

'You have a better theory, perhaps?'

'No transport,' he said. 'You need an escort. I can't spare you one. That is the end of the matter. Please go now.'

I left at once, undismayed. The Commissaire is an underling and I wanted to save my breath for the Governor who sent word that afternoon requesting my immediate presence at the *Seraya*. I made him wait a full thirty minutes, which Wendell told me later was ill-advised.

The Governor is a very different bag from the Commissaire. I know the type from Syria. A large, skulking Albanian, he bullies his subordinates and enriches himself madly while he can, accustomed to the vagaries of imperial favour. Throughout our talk he nervously twitched his head over his shoulder, a tic, perhaps, or else he fears spies, and after the usual pleasantries he questioned me again about my intentions.

This time I was much more direct. After briskly outlining the historical purpose of my journey, I said that I'd be ready to leave in about ten days' time, once I had collected together my stores, and that I would dispense with an official escort as I could well afford to arrange my own protection.

'Anyway,' I went on, holding him in my sights and speaking the words carefully, well schooled by Dr Wendell, 'an escort is hardly necessary as I'm unlikely to encounter any trouble. That's right, isn't it? I mean, it's all quite quiet at present, I understand.'

From his accelerated twitchings, I knew that he was caught. The Porte vehemently denies as slander any rumours of impending revolt in its dominions and one risks incarceration as an *agent provocateur* for breathing the slightest hint of insubordination amongst the massing tribes.

'It's quiet, yes,' said the Governor unhappily, 'but there are brigands, you know, in this part of the world. An armed escort is therefore . . . desirable. As the Commissaire has explained to you, it's all very difficult. We can't spare one right now.'

'They say in London,' I replied, wide-eyed with innocence, 'that Mohammed 'Ali Pasha, the Vali at San'ā, has restored order throughout the *vilayet* and that the roads are safe for even the most timid traveller. You wouldn't wish me, surely, to inform them otherwise? The Vali is a very old friend.'

He didn't know what he wished. Plucking frantically at his coat-sleeve and swivelling his eyes around, he agreed that most of the robbers had gone, true, but the odd one or two might remain. Freebooters, as it were. One couldn't lock up an entire population. Where would one put them all, for one thing?

'I can deal with the odd one or two,' I said, and judged it time to leave before I laughed outright at his discomfort. At the top of the rickety stairs I paused long enough to hear him explode like one of his Maxim guns and vent his rage on the orderly who had lounged on a couch throughout our brief meeting, picking his teeth.

The Mutessarif has amply confirmed my opinion of the Turk. My friends at the Foreign Office are at pains to point out that while he has certain qualities which give him credit – he's dignified, hospitable to strangers, courageous as a soldier, moderately kind to animals, hard-working, fond of children, and honest in trade – he has a number of serious defects which render him unreliable as an ally; to wit, he's backward, cruel to subject races, abjectly submissive in the face of Government orders, mistrustful of his own shadow, and extremely slow-witted. You have only to dig him a pit and he'll fall into it. Dr Wendell says I underestimate him: we'll see which one of us is right.

The rest of my time has been spent with Yūsuf in the bazaars. He won't let me pay one piastre more than I need. Camp equipment, bedding, medicines, and a fair part of my provisions I purchased at Harrods, so we seek only miscellaneous stores. I've hired four baggage camels from a cousin of the mayor, somewhat ragged specimens which I need for crossing the Tihāmah and the lower foothills, after which I shall procure myself some mules and send the camels back to Hodeidah.

For myself I seek a good strong mare and may also want some men. I have my eye on a band of Zaranik tribesmen encamped near the brackish wells outside the gates. A lawless lot under Sheikh Mohammed Yahya Fashīk, they're reputed to be very good shots. I'll take Wendell's advice on whether their 'protection' will be necessary.

I don't envy the Vice-Consul his posting: it's like Jiddah without the street-lamps and verminous to a degree, especially in the native quarters beyond the walls where the thatched huts and impoverished compounds recall the sights and smells of East Africa. To make matters worse, one can't turn a street corner without falling into Turkish soldiery hunting for some amusement which, apart from wrestling, the odd performance of the garrison's atrocious band, and carousing half the night in the casino dressed in their nightshirts, is pretty thin on the ground.

I'll be glad to breathe the cleaner air of the mountains, and leave these Turkish monkey dances behind.

30 December 1910

I've seen Mr Fergusson in the bazaar. I'm certain it was he, though dressed in Arab guise. Those black bushy brows. His skin cracked and tanned to the colour of a native's. Or did I dream him myself? I no longer know what to believe.

Yūsuf and I were arguing with a merchant over the purchase of some cloth he needs for a new suit of clothes when I caught sight of that unmistakable profile across the square. He'd moved from the covered shade into a slat of brilliant sunlight and for a few seconds stood illuminated, inspecting some books laid out on the ground. I know it was he. My heart knocked. I must be angry with him still at the manner of our parting. I called his name. 'Mr Fergusson,' I said, 'I thought you went to Musawwaʿ.' He shot me a look of the purest alarm. Oh yes, I know it was he. One can't mistake those eyes. He'd grown a beard, his face looked darker than before but I would stake my life that it was Mr Fergusson.

The merchant, fearing to lose a valued customer, tugged at my sleeve. I turned to shake him off and, when I looked again across the square, the space was bare. The bookseller dozed cross-legged on his platform. Flies swarmed in the air. Mr Fergusson had disappeared.

I sent Yūsuf to look for him. It wasn't seemly to go myself and yet I knew his quest was vain. That only I could seek him out. I did so wish to talk to him again, to find out how he was keeping and whether he thought of me at all.

With Yūsuf despatched on his errand, I crossed the square to ask the bookseller if the stranger's fancy had been drawn to any book in particular. He showed a copy of the *Qur'ān* (a most surprising choice), with beautifully worked chapter headings, which I bought as a keepsake for the price required.

Downcast at having lost again what I had found, I returned to my house where I took my palliasse up to the roof and Mr Fergusson's book and watched a group of noisy urchins poking sticks at a ragged object floating in the stagnant waters of the harbour. It looked like the hind legs of a donkey. I felt a sudden yearning for Maunton and my dark Northumbrian hills. The sooner I start this journey the better I shall be. The time for waiting is past.

1 January 1911

God willing, the die is cast: I leave in three days' time. I'm not entirely prepared but Wendell says that if I delay much longer the whole shooting party will erupt and my journey of exploration will get no further than the gates of Hodeidah.

Armed brigands have appeared in various quarters in the mountains, to snipe at the Turk and harry the post which is rumoured to be stuck at Sūq el-Khamīs. Most of the tribes of the highlands, all Zeidi Moslems, have declared for the Imam and even the Sunnis of the plains are festering. The notorious Boni Pasha, principal Sheikh of the Zeidis and one time ally of the Turk, has escaped from San'ā and fled to join the Imam at his mountain fortress of Shehārah. Expecting trouble, the garrisons at Yerīm and Ta'izz have sent urgent appeals to the Hodeidah authorities for reinforcements, requests which cannot be met for lack of men. If there is to be a revolt, the Turks have been caught with their trousers down, in spite of all the signs.

Far worse for my own situation, the Mutessarif has branded me a British spy, sent by His Majesty's Government to curry favour with the rebels. I thought he'd looked askance at my story. Unable to accept historical curiosity as sufficient motive to drive me across the mountains into the desert wastes beyond, he pays no credence to my intended explorations.

All this was told to me at the Consulate where I had been invited by Dr Wendell and his wife to attend a small At Home on New Year's Eve. I'd thought to decline but Wendell's dragoman had hinted darkly that the Consul wanted to see me urgently and couldn't visit my house because I'm under constant surveillance from the Turks. I've seen them lounging across the way, two, sometimes three soldiers, who make no attempt at concealment and pester Yūsuf for information on my movements.

As soon as I arrived, Mary Wendell said, 'He'll see you now. In his study. Quick, we don't want the others to suspect anything amiss.'

I found her husband in a state of extreme agitation. His words tripped over each other as he outlined for me the political situation with its thickening intrigues.

'What's to be done?' I asked, alarmed.

'You must get rid of them.'

'My guards? But how? They're acting under orders. I can't simply shoo them away.'

'This calls, Miss Grace, for a little ingenuity. I've got an idea I think'll do the trick.'

His plan was good. I wished that Uncle Gerald could see me now as we plotted my escape from under the very noses of the Turks. (Uncle Gerald it was who gave me the first taste of the life I have embraced. The two would understand each other well.)

When we were quite agreed, he looked at me fondly. 'You know, my dear,' he said, wiping away what looked suspiciously like a tear, 'I do believe that if I had an ounce more nerve, I'd go with you myself.'

At this he blew his nose loudly and called for his wife to introduce me to the company which had been invited at short notice to provide the necessary witnesses for our charade. The ill-assorted guests included a Romanian with an unpronounceable name from the audit department; a Mr Patterji, exporter of coffee and hides, and his mouse of a wife who tittered through her hands; a travelling salesman called Jones who specialized in carved ivories and other African knick-knacks; a French engineer by the name of Chavagnac prospecting the railway line up to Hajeilah; and the shady German who had disembarked with me from the Khedivial mailship. The latter

introduced himself as Count Otto von Preissinger and thereafter sat in a corner by himself.

Their paltry conversations I parried as well as I could. Jones
was likeable in a mercantile sort of way, with a fund of stories
he unpacked from his kitbag and laid on the floor for our
approval. He'd spent some time in Harar and become
embroiled in the arms traffic centred on the port of Jibuti. The
French, it seems, are up to their necks in it.

When the engineer joined us, the conversation turned to the
railway planned to link the new harbour at Ras el-Kethīb to
Hodeidah and San'ā. After more than a year of arguments,
they still can't agree on a route. I expect it'll go the way of most
Turkish innovations and, once the track has lurched a few
miles into the desert, they'll all lose heart.

At this point the discussion grew quite animated, so much
so that I overlooked Wendell's signal until he positively waved
at me. Jones saw him first; said he thought the doctor wanted a
word with me. Pulling myself together, I uttered a moan,
threw my hands to my head and sank untidily to the floor.

I must have acted too well because they bunched and jostled
around me until I gasped in truth for breath. The nights on the
coast are sticky as the days. After I had counted a full minute I
opened my eyes to a grotesque canopy of faces leering above
my head.

Mrs Wendell cleared me a path and helped me to a chair. 'A
chill,' she said. 'You look deathly pale, Miss Grace. Were you
out in the gardens?'

I nodded.

'A breeding place for fevers. No one sits there who does not
succumb.'

'Blackwater fever,' exclaimed Jones. 'She's turned yellow.
Good God. Or could it be cholera?'

The engineer looked at me nervously.

'It's just a fever,' said Mrs Wendell. 'We'll take her home at
once.'

I murmured helpless thanks. Her concern was expressed with such sincerity I guessed she was not party to her husband's plan but, as they helped me down the stairs, she whispered in my ear, 'God speed, you shall not go alone,' and Dr Wendell winked at me.

She said goodbye at the door. Dr Wendell called for his *kavass*, who strode before us with a lantern. I followed next, half-dragged, half-carried by the Vice-Consul and his dragoman, with Jones keeping his distance on the outer flank. Some way behind us, in the dark, stumbled the Turkish soldiers sent to spy on me.

We made an odd procession. A night wind from the sea caught us in the cross-streets; we heard the wailing of fractious children and the watchmen's long-drawn howls and I near fainted again at the ghostly strangeness of it all.

Now I must bide my time and write my letters home – the last for several months – which Dr Wendell has promised to convey personally to the captain of the mailsteamer. They'll send my meals over from the Consulate, the broth of invalids in case the Turks should wonder at my appetite, and maybe Mary Wendell will sit with me to pass the hours.

I've promised Yūsuf an extra week's pay if we reach the mountains as planned. He grinned and drew a line across his throat.

4 January 1911

The ruse has worked. I leave at nightfall. By noon yesterday my Turkish guard had dwindled to one, a mere lad who drew with a stick in the dust and picked his teeth with splinters from the same. Today even he has gone, so they must have picked up rumours, spread by Dr Wendell, that my fever worsens by the hour. Soon, it's said, I shall be carried out of the house feet first and lain to rest in the little cemetery beyond the town, a

visitor who stayed too long. One shouldn't laugh at death but I
wonder what the Turks would make of my obituary.

Yesterday afternoon Yūsuf strapped my boxes into bundles
of reeds found in the granary, had them loaded into carts at the
front door and packed off to market under the less than beady
eyes of the Turkish guard. A more complicated subterfuge
were bound to fail, but such a simple operation, conducted in
broad daylight, raised not the slightest hint of suspicion.
Forced to leave my best things behind, I've given Mary
Wendell a full inventory in case the Mutessarif should attempt
some double-dealing of his own.

After my boxes had gone, Yūsuf went too. I watched him
from an upper window, fearful he might overplay his hand.
Bearing his roll of belongings under one arm, a large bundle of
wilting *kat* leaves under the other, he sauntered across the
street to exchange a few words with the guard and waved
airily in the direction of Aden. He's left me a suit of his clothes
and no one shall remark an ill-dressed Arab youth who leaves
this house as soon as darkness falls.

Since his departure, time drags slowly by. Mary Wendell,
good soul, paid me a call this morning with her daughter to tell
me that the last of my arrangements are made. They've
procured a guide to take me over the Tihāmah plains to the
foothills, a distance of some thirty miles which we'll cross in
darkness to escape detection and the worst effects of the heat.
The girl Elizabeth gave me a present which touched me
greatly: a volume of poems by Tennyson (not my favourites)
in which she had neatly written my name. I'll carry it on my
wanderings to remind me of the good folk left behind.

In three hours I'll be gone. The sun sinks into a bank of
clouds above the horizon; soon it will be snuffed without the
gorgeous glow of evening. To my right, the houses of the
town sweep round the bay and I listen, for the last time, to the
sea breaking restlessly against the moles. The house is swept
and bare, except for the few crates stacked against the wall.

There'll be no moon tonight, nor stars by which to navigate my route. I'll catch some rest to fortify my valour and my nerves.

6 January 1911

My journey promises to be a strange one; nothing is quite what it seems and, just when my plans are laid firm, the ground beneath me shifts and I find myself heading off in the opposite direction, sometimes literally. It's all most disconcerting, as if the compass tells me north when I am heading south. In all senses of the word I travel through uncharted territory with Mr Fergusson at my side. Actually, that's not strictly true. He has a most annoying habit of taking the lead in this expedition, forcing me to follow more meekly in his wake.

Our escape from Hodeidah bears all the hallmarks of a bad dream, a dream from which one wakes to find the dream continues, as in a hall of mirrors where what one sees is but the reflection of a reflection, and a poor one at that.

After darkness had fallen on the evening of 4 January, I changed into Yūsuf's spare clothes and blacked my face, curiously apprehensive at the schoolgirl escapade ahead. The house was full of scurryings. Shadows slipped across the steps. Several times I thought I heard a baby crying in an upper room. Outside, the street was empty, thank God, and silent except for the distant shouts of Turkish revelry in the casino.

No one so much as glanced at me as I made my way towards the meeting point with Yūsuf, a merchant's house on the outskirts of the town where my baggage camels were to await me, ready loaded for our night-time crossing of the Tihāmah. I found the compound without difficulty and entered hopefully to discover no Yūsuf, no baggage camels, no guide, no Arab mare (purchased, I might say, at exorbitant cost), only a barren of bad-tempered mules. I could have wept my shame at having entrusted my person and all my worldly possessions to a man who was plainly a thief.

In a fit of pique I flung my headgear to the ground. This sneaking Arab had robbed me of more than my stores. Beset by unaccustomed failure, I turned towards the gates and had almost left the compound when a long low whistle, like a night owl's, caught me off guard. Startled, I peered around. An unknown Arab loomed out of the far corner. He looked a most truculent ruffian, dressed in a merchant's long black robes. I spoke to him sharply, in his own tongue. He made no reply. From this distance, without a moon, I couldn't see his face, but I had plainly walked into a trap. These Arabs of the town would sooner murder you than bid you good day. Angry at the way I had been treated, I stood my ground.

The man advanced towards me, flapping his cloak with an air of menace. He had a rolling gait that struck me straight away as false; I'd never seen an Arab walk like that before. The closer he got, the more I wanted to run. Only when he was almost upon me did I discover his identity. It was, of course, Mr Fergusson.

'You're late,' he said peremptorily. 'We must be gone.'

'We?' I echoed, taken aback. 'I wasn't expecting you.'

'You'll need a guide. Didn't Wendell tell you it was all arranged?'

'Indeed he did, but I'd assumed a local man.'

'I told him not to tell. He talks too much.'

'I like Dr Wendell.'

'So do I. We understand each other. That doesn't alter the fact of his talking.'

'What are you doing here? I thought you'd gone to Mus-awwa'.'

'We haven't time for explanations.'

'But where are my things?'

'They've gone ahead. Your man has too. We'll meet up later

in the mountains. We're safer on our own, providing we leave now. Are you armed?'

I nodded.

'Good man,' he said. 'I'm off. Come if you like, or stay if you prefer.'

'My boxes . . . '

'Damn your boxes.'

'They contain valuable equipment. I can't abandon them like this.'

'I'm sure you can't, Miss Grace. If you'll not come with me, I'll see you get them back. I thought you had the mettle for adventure.'

He looked at me darkly, the spider at his fly, and from the rush of blood to my heart I knew I'd step into his parlour, come what may.

'What's it to be?' he asked, most casually.

I said he'd left me no choice. I couldn't hire myself another guide at this hour of night, nor could I locate Yūsuf alone. I'd have to go with him. At this he merely nodded and remarked it were not before time.

And so we left Hodeidah by the back streets, which Mr Fergusson knows extremely well, mounted on mules and keeping a watch for stray Turkish eyes. We took a wide sweep around the barracks, passed the walled garden and the tennis courts on our left and the white crossless tombs of the European cemetery on our right, and found ourselves in less than fifteen minutes out in the wide, dark plain.

We weren't the only travellers that night. As the moon was hid by clouds, we stuck close to the main route and passed at frequent intervals the ghosts of camel-trains, bringing their loads of *kat* and fodder down from the highlands, hulking shapes that emerged out of the darkness to greet us and disappear.

The sandy ground was rippled by the wind and dotted with hummocks of *bokār* grass, while further inland we passed through thickets of trees, date palms, I think, and the odd screw-pine. I couldn't observe more closely because of the gloom and, anyway, the circumstances surrounding our flight were hardly conducive to scientific observations. One part of me was alarmed at the direction I appeared to be taking, the other elated at being so rudderless in this ocean of sand, following my nose and Mr Fergusson's whim.

Our first day on the road was bad indeed. By sunrise, we had reached Bājil at the outer skirts of the Tihāmah, a town to which we gave wide berth on account of the Turkish fort above a hillock. We excited no interest (the wind was raining dust) and though I wanted for refreshments Mr Fergusson decided that we should press on to the foothills, to make the most of our advantage. We continued for several hours, with only fetid water to drink. Every bone in my seat ached from the dreadful stumblings of my mule, a very stupid animal, and in the burnished heat it felt as if a hammer struck my skull from the inside. The light was so sharp I kept eyes shut much of the time and nearly fell off.

At last, thank God, when we had started up a wide valley some ten miles across, Mr Fergusson indicated that we could rest awhile in the scanty shade afforded by a clump of tamarisk trees. I had so stiffened from the ride I could barely dismount, and the provisions he produced from our solitary pack animal gave little cause for celebration: parched Arab bread, tough enough for shoe leather, a flask of cold *qishr* tasting of barley water and a bowl of rancid *ghi*. I looked on the bright side, however, and felt a little cheered. We had successfully cocked a snook at the Mutessarif who must be twitching like an epileptic right now, a real St Vitus's dance, and like a babe I had stumbled those first tottering steps towards my goal.

But oh, as we took up position on either side of our tree, I did so miss my old ways, sitting with my trusted followers around the camp fire, an honorary man among men. Here, I'm more of a stranger than I had anticipated and must rely on such as Dr Wendell and Mr Fergusson for help. I do not care to take another's orders and yet I must, and humbly, if I am to succeed.

Mr Fergusson was not in a talkative mood. He wrapped his cloak around his head, stretched out full-length on the ground, and fell asleep. Discountenanced, I did likewise and must have slept for two or three hours because, when I awoke, the shadows had swung round so that I lay directly in the sun. Instead of feeling refreshed, the knocking within my head had merely intensified.

To my chagrin, Mr Fergusson was already awake. He squatted on a rock some twenty feet away, Arab-style, eyeing me with dispassionate intent. I wished I looked a little better for his inspection. My hair, knotted into a coil to keep it secure under my headcloth, felt like a tangled bird's nest and my face was larded with grime. For once I envied Jane the neatness of her features. Everything about me leans towards the generous, as if the Good Lord endowed me with all his gifts then spoilt the effect by adding a little extra for good measure. As for my clothes . . . I was dressed as a simple Arab boy and there was nothing I could do about that.

Whether I passed muster, I cannot say. After he had finished staring at me, he stood up and said we had dallied long enough. We should get on our way if we were to reach Hajeilah by nightfall. I resented the implication that he had waited for me.

We camped in fact before Hajeilah because my mule stumbled off the road and cut its leg on a thorn bush. Mr Fergusson was all for abandoning the creature in the valley but responded to my argument that, as we'd need another beast to carry us on to Yūsuf and the baggage camels, a wounded animal to exchange was better than none. I refused his offer, made after I had walked a good mile, to ride his mule in his stead and was a little annoyed that the offer was promptly withdrawn.

The road we travelled had swung to the south-east, between the mountains of Jebel Masār and the spur of Jebel Bura'. Flat-topped acacias clung to the dry river bed and sandstorms spiralled up the *wādi* like squally showers, filling the air with dust and deadening the light. Apart from the broad back of Mr Fergusson some way ahead, I had little on which to set my sights, and was relieved therefore to halt in a straggling native village where we purchased a mount from a surly muleteer who gave me a shilling for my wounded animal, judging we were in no position to argue its worth.

We ate some chicken at a roadside café, so stringy it might have died from old age. My appetite was somewhat disturbed by the sound of loud thumpings from the next table: a Negroid sort of fellow was eating a sheep's head by first splitting its skull against the wall, a gruesome set of table manners to which Mr Fergusson paid no attention. As we rode out of the village, I looked longingly at the thatched sheds for travellers but knew that to stay there would risk discovery. Such places in any case simply crawl with fleas that hop from one traveller to the next in true democracy of the road.

I shall pass over quickly that first night spent in the open five miles or more before Hajeilah. There was an unfortunate contretemps between the two of us, about which the less said the better. It concerned my tent which had been sent on with Yūsuf's advance party. Not as an oversight, I might add, but because Mr Fergusson does not believe in tents. They are not necessary. We bivouacked on the hard ground and left before dawn, still not speaking to each other.

The changing landscape broke slowly into our mutual coldness and, though we continued to exchange few words, our silence was more companionable and Mr Fergusson took to whistling snatches of the more popular arias. We left the plain at daybreak, crossed two steep ravines and halted for a scant thirty minutes at the village of Obal, where we ate some bread dipped in camel's milk floating with globules of *ghi*.

As Hajeilah bustled with troops, their tents pitched among

the squat stone buildings, we cut behind the town and after passing through well-cultivated farmland we found ourselves in a narrow gorge with rock-faces some eighty feet in height. The air grew hotter by the minute and the presence of huge boulders forced us to dismount and pick our way through the stones.

The travellers we met were mainly farmers and a small caravan of footsore camels. No one spoke beyond the briefest courtesies. There hung between us a brooding wariness, each man uncertain who was friend or foe, and I had the curious impression of travelling among a people who have stopped the ordinary business of living as they wait for the slaughter to begin. I expect I'm merely romanticizing the *status quo*: these tribes are never peaceful for long.

Eventually we passed under a huge boulder that had fallen across the ravine and, a few miles further on, past pleasant mimosa trees, we left the river bed to follow a track that zigzagged perilously up the mountain flank, quite outrageous in parts. The road bears witness to Turkish ingenuity but not, I must report, to any notion of Turkish husbandry. Once built, it has been left to fall apart; its usefulness as a troop route is severely limited. The surface has eroded so badly it's quite unfit for vehicular traffic and one has only to stand further up the road to crash down boulders on the heads of one's enemies below. I don't expect the Turks have thought of that.

The air grew cooler as we climbed sharply and I marvelled at the terraces that clung tenaciously to the near-perpendicular ravines, their contours geometrically precise. Even Mr Fergusson seemed awed by this majestic landscape and stopped his whistling. As for myself, I feared I might succumb to vertigo and kept my eyes on the track which climbed ever upwards, traversing pockets of verdure although the late summer rains are long since past.

We came across a covey of black-headed chikore, *Caccabis melanocephala*, which I pointed out to my companion. Despite a certain sharpness of eye, he isn't very familiar with the wildlife around here which seems odd for a naturalist. I can't help feeling that the British Museum has chosen the wrong man for the job. He said he preferred beetles to birds and went on ahead.

We halted near Wāsil on a patch of flat ground overhanging the abyss, too narrow for a tent so its absence went unmourned. Now is not the time to discover that one walks in one's sleep.

Supper was a cheerful affair, balanced on a rock near the lip. We caught the last rays of the sun and both glowed yellow in its evening light. Mr Fergusson produced from his saddle-bag a bottle of claret, much travelled but surprisingly drinkable, and became quite loquacious. His deep voice echoed across the peaks – and his laugh: I've never seen him so good-humoured before. The mountains suit him better than the plains; he's lost his boorishness and now exudes a sense of physical ease that sets my hairs on end.

He's led an odd sort of life. I can't see its attractions. For four long years he's chased his tail up and down the coasts of Arabïa, stopping briefly at Aden where he worked for Luke Thomas & Co., shipping merchants and jacks of all trades. From the description of his duties it seems he was some kind of clerk, though it's hard to picture him sitting at a desk. His knees would scarcely fit and his temperament is quite opposed to the careful business of clerking.

Disliking Aden as much as I did (he said it stank of unwashed Arabs and the second sons of Empire), he left hurriedly to try his hand at something else, going first to Berbera across the Gulf of Aden and then to Zeila which he used as a base to make several sorties inland, getting as far as Harar. He had not, he said, come across Jones.

When we had finished our meal he lay back on the rock, quite content to lie abandoned at my feet, and I was glad for once of his silence. I found myself wanting to touch him, a most peculiar sensation. Though he's undoubtedly a strange companion, his very strangeness sparks my interest. I find myself agreeing with him in preference to my own opinions. He has a theory, for instance, that one must travel unencumbered by any sort of baggage, by which he means more than my camping equipment. One must be free, he says, to take what comes.

I tried to tell him about my own journey and how I intend to reach Māreb to disprove once and for all the ancient city's connection with Sheba. He took my hand and said with a half-smile, 'Don't you think, my dear Miss Grace, that myths can be more telling than the truth?' I smiled in my turn. Some things are better left to me.

As he lay on the rock, I asked about his people, a subject on which he is especially reticent.

'I have a sister,' he said. 'Her name is Isobel.'

'Is she married?'

'She lives alone in Glasgow. That's my home too.'

'Anyone else?' I enquired.

He raised himself on one elbow. 'I have an aunt in London,' he said slowly, 'if that's what you mean.'

I blushed and talked about myself, the many journeys I have made. I wasn't meaning to boast but travel is an interest we share. He wondered if it weren't too dangerous, for a woman alone. I told him that although I have often encountered situations of great personal danger I have always emerged unhurt. 'I'm sure you have, Miss Grace,' he said. 'It'd be a very brave man who'd dare to cross swords with you.'

I like him enormously and hope I enjoy his esteem. He treats me with bantering good humour and blows a bit hot and cold, but if one scratches a little beneath the bushel of his black looks one discovers a decent heart after all.

We talked until darkness fell then F. went off for a walk, saying he couldn't sleep. He left me at my journal which I write by the flickering beam of a lantern, wrapped in a sheet because the temperature has dropped alarmingly and I am stiff with cold. Tomorrow we shall head for the village of Hajarah, from whence we'll get word to Yūsuf who has taken the longer route up the Wādi Sihām.

I long to surround myself with my things. I hear dogs barking and see the twinkling lights of villages several thousand feet above my head. I look forward with a new heart to the morrow, whatever it may bring.

7 January 1911

Our journey today has been simply marvellous; my one regret is that Father could not accompany us. He would have gasped aloud at the magical splendour of the landscape, its jagged ranges all jostled together and fading into the palest blue.

I'm used to the shifting dunes and flat, stony horizons of the desert that shrink one's significance to the merest speck of dust within the world's vast emptiness, but here we soar as eagles, closer to heaven than earth with all its dusty cares. Had we less compelling business in hand, I'd set up camp for a fortnight to make some sketches that would surely delight in their bold cragginess.

Soon after Wāsil we took Wendell's advice and cut across the mountains, away from the sights of Ottoman guns upon the dizzy heights of Masār. On the surface all seems calm, so calm I wonder if this talk of revolution is still not premature.

As my map has proved singularly unreliable, we hired ourselves a guide, a local boy, afflicted with a hunchback and a keen, rat-like face, who trotted along first one path then the next in ever-widening circles until I wondered if he weren't a *jinni* in human form sent to lead us astray. Mr Fergusson had a more prosaic explanation: he surmised the lad was a simpleton and spoke to him sharply in a vernacular Arabic that would bring credit to a camel driver. Thereafter we progressed more or less in a straight line, across jasmine-fringed slopes, past coffee terraces and giddy ravines, then up the perilous track towards the windswept wastes of Hajarah pass.

Rock pigeons abounded and crows, of course, and once I heard the glorious song of *Pseudacanthis yemenensis* which looks like a sparrow and sings like a skylark.

By mid-afternoon we caught sight of our goal: the tall houses of Hajarah perched on the highest point above the precipice. Here our young guide planted his bare feet firmly on either side of the path and resolutely refused to take us further in case he were blamed for whatever bad luck the Unbelievers are certain to bring. As Mr Fergusson declared his conduct had forfeited any reward, I took it upon myself to disburse some coins and a small hunting knife, at which the boy smiled for the first time, the smile of a petrified rat, and ran away as fast as his short legs would carry him.

Rather to my concern, Mr Fergusson had ridden on ahead and passed from view when I entered the outlying part of the village built on a separate spur. The men thronging my route were true mountaineers, lighter-skinned and altogether more wiry than lowland folk, their skin stained blue from the indigo dyes of their kilts. Each sported the menacing blade of a curved *jambiyah* thrust into his waistband and carried all manner of arms. I felt uneasy to ride unguarded through their hostile stares.

In situations such as this it's advisable to field one's most natural front and so I continued calmly through the village, noting its prosperous air. The houses, built like watchtowers of interlocking stones, were freshly daubed with whitewash, straight lines interspersed with zigzags: a child's idea of decoration. From upper windows poked the unveiled heads of the womenfolk, and curious children who looked, from a distance, well fed. At least the women responded to my greetings, waving and pointing their fingers at me with much laughter and jostling for position.

On reaching the end of the spur, I halted my beast in some

consternation. The track ahead dipped into a hollow and climbed again in rough-hewn steps to disappear between the walls of the main village, a most imposing structure formed by the contiguous base of the outer houses which rose a hundred feet or more. My thoughts, however, were far from architecture. Mr Fergusson astride his mule was at that point climbing the steep steps towards the gates, his long legs brushing the ground, blissfully unaware of a heavily-armed welcome party that had formed at the top of the steps, seven or eight young men, more ferocious even than the scrawny pirates who surrounded me.

I held my breath as a village elder thrust himself to the fore, a beak-nosed fellow wrapped in a voluminous kaftan the colour of a kingfisher. The mountain fastness fell suddenly silent, as if the children had been taken away, and all waited to see what would happen next. Were we to be welcomed or shot? In all that silence I heard the far-distant cry of a bird, and thought, a trifle blasphemously, of the entry into Jerusalem.

Mr Fergusson, I'm glad to say, quickly mastered the situation. A yard or more from the group he looked upwards for the first time, gave a sort of bow then slid from his mule. His gun belt he unbuckled and laid at the kaftan's feet. The two sniffed at each other like dogs uncertain of their territory then Mr Fergusson bent down, removed his pistol and held it out to the old man who looked cautiously down its barrel and nodded courteously. At this a cheer rang out through the mountains: we had found ourselves among friends.

Anxious to rejoin my companion, I spurred my mule down the track and up again through the massive wooden gates to the village where I was immediately caught in a welcoming stampede. We squeezed as best we could through the stony passageways, Mr Fergusson's head bobbing up and down above the throng some way in front. He turned to smile encouragement and shouted something to me I could not catch. Just as I feared I might be crushed against the walls we

gave a last, desperate heave and forced our way out of the
warren into the central square, a sloping plot of waste ground
on which stood a mosque, a spreading cactus, and a house
more elaborately decorated than the rest into which Mr
Fergusson disappeared without so much as a backward glance
for me.

The worst was yet to come. As I fought my way to the front
door I was suddenly engulfed in a swarm of screeching women
who emerged from the house, all talking at once and jabbing at
my clothes. It was immediately apparent that Mr Fergusson
had told all. Instead of being conducted with the other notables
to the *mafraj* at the top of the house, I was led like a prize turkey
to the women's quarters and very firmly put in my place.

With much girlish laughter they stripped me of my boy's
attire and draped me in a sort of shapeless tunic, dark blue, and
baggy trousers that tapered towards the ankles. I looked like
something out of *'Ali Baba*. My toilette completed to the
satisfaction of my assembled audience, they flooded me with
questions. What country was I from? Did I live in a house as
large as theirs? Had I been blessed by many children? How
many, exactly?

To introduce myself properly I produced a much-loved
photograph of home taken on the West Terrace at Maunton.
Mother, wearing a rather splendid hat, sits regally next to a
stone urn, one hand resting on a cane. Jane, looking unusually
solemn (she had a headache, I think), kneels by her side, her
striped skirts spread across the steps, one arm around each of
our nephews who grin cheekily at the camera. Father and
Edward stand back to back as if they have just fallen out. The
group was taken during my Syrian travels which explains my
absence from the party.

This photograph was snatched from my hands and passed
from one to the next. I tried to snatch it back. Eventually it fell
into the hands of a small, sharp-eyed woman, older than the
rest, whose girth would encompass several of me. Pointing at

Jane and the boys, she asked if these were my only children, having obviously mistaken Jane for myself. The room was dark and, if one hasn't seen a likeness before, I suppose one can't appreciate its image must be exact. We did, in any case, look a little alike: the photograph did not do her justice.

I explained that Jane was my younger sister and that the boys belonged to another sister, Ida, also absent from the group. She found my Syrian speech hard to comprehend. With a shrug, she slipped the photograph into the folds of her skirts and that was the last I saw of it. I protested, of course, but as I was sorely outnumbered must soon bow to the inevitable.

We are, it seems, lodged in the house of the 'Aqil, or Headman; the sharp-eyed woman is his number-one wife. I asked to be taken up to Mr Fergusson, which caused flutters of concern. The men were chewing *kat* and could not be disturbed. Besides, they hadn't sent for me. It was a galling experience and relations between us quickly became strained. The women developed an annoying habit of clutching me tightly round the wrists, though whether to demonstrate their affection or to prevent my escape was not made clear. They couldn't answer my questions about the imminence of war, nor had I much to say in answer to theirs. I had no children. I lived in a house a little larger than theirs (I didn't say how large) and I came from England, a country of which they had never heard; one asked if it were close to Medina.

Just when I had begun to despair, a lad appeared at the door and summoned me upstairs. We climbed the narrow cork-screwed steps, dark as a dungeon, up to a room near the top of the house where I found Mr Fergusson, alone. He appeared not to notice my dress, or anything, for that matter. His eyes had glazed over, an effect I attributed to an over-indulgence in *kat*.

'Look here,' he said, 'I'm dreadfully sorry. You're to sleep here.'

'What's wrong with that? The room looks fine to me. Anything is better than being cooped up with the women. It really wasn't fair. I thought you'd forgotten me.'

'You don't understand. You won't be alone, you know. I hadn't thought it through. I mean, dammit, it wasn't intentional.'

'What do you mean, I won't be alone? With whom must I share my lodgings?'

He looked so crestfallen that the truth dawned.

'You mean, sir, I'm to share it with you.'

'I said we're man and wife. It seemed the simplest explanation. We'd be stoned if they thought anything different. Miss Grace, you really must accept my apologies. I'm truly sorry. I can always sleep outside. Or somewhere.'

He looked it, too. I said briskly, 'We've shared the open air together, before now. This room is large enough for two. I'll just pretend you're not here.'

'You're not angry with me?'

'Oh, I wouldn't say I was angry. When one travels, you know, one must be free to take whatever comes.'

The shadows hid my smiles. We made ourselves comfortable with rough woollen blankets brought to our room by the boy and, when he had left us, took up position at either end of the room. Mr Fergusson cocooned himself in his coverings, bade me a gruff good night and quickly fell asleep.

My mind is much too vibrant for sleep. I write this by the fitful glare of an oil lamp which spits and hisses in its corner and throws peculiar shadows around the room, listening to the steady rise and fall of Mr Fergusson's deep slumbers, sounds which amplify until they fill the space that lies between us, the space between a man and his wife, and I think: No, I mustn't think that, such thoughts are wildly misplaced. I shall say only it was maybe not so wrong of Mr Fergusson to make his claims and that in lying one can sometimes speak the truth.

Goodnight, dear James, and may the Good Lord keep us in peace.

8 January 1911

Mr Fergusson travels most casually in a fashion I can't decide whether to admire or condemn. On waking this morning I found him ready dressed, one hand thrust into my money belt which I had placed on the floor close to my head. His rustlings must have awakened me because the room was cast in dusky gloom.

'What are you doing?' I asked. 'Mr Fergusson, please. Those are my things.'

He jumped for his gun, a reflex action, I trust. He would not murder me, I think. Taking hold of his manners, he knelt beside my bed and said he wished to borrow money. As I was sleeping soundly, he thought he'd bother with the asking later.

'Where are you going?'

'I'm off to meet Yūsuf near Idz. We'll need some mules to bring our stores back to Hajarah.'

'I'll come with you,' I said, attempting to rise as modestly as circumstances allowed. 'The mules, is that what the money's for?'

He nodded. 'I'll go alone. It's quicker that way.'

'I thought we were partners.'

'We are. You'll get the money back. Soon enough I'll have more than I need.'

I gave him the money, of course. He claims to possess a letter of credit to the Ottoman Bank in San'ā, so I'll not make a loss on the transaction, but I can't help wondering at his imprudence in travelling so short of ready cash, and mine in letting him go, though not before he had written out a bill setting down the exact monies owed.

I lay abed some time, anxious and annoyed that I should always be the one left behind. If he needed money, he should have asked me yesterday. And why must I stay here alone, with only the blessed women for company?

At least I have had plenty of opportunity to become acquainted with their primitive ways. Although these houses are remarkable architecturally, the living conditions have barely progressed beyond the Stone Age: their kitchen is a poky cavern in which one's eyes smart from the acrid smoke and, as for their sanitary arrangements, well, the best one can say is that they are economical. The house has several 'bathrooms', each built above the other and containing a large earthenware water jar covered with a cloth, and two raised pedestals above a hole in the floor, its solid contents dropping through a single walled shaft to an excrement chamber on the ground floor. One imagines it must be swilled out occasionally but this is plainly not the time of year.

All living rooms are furnished in basically the same spartan manner: threadbare carpets, shabby cushions, alcoves and gypsum shelves crammed with their few belongings. The rough plaster walls, decorated with endearingly crude bas-relief, are sorely in need of a lick of whitewash. But the views from my narrow windows are quite magnificent.

After a light lunch of sorghum pancakes with the women, I could stand my captivity no longer and took a walk through the village, dogged by a taggle of boisterous children who made me feel like the Pied Piper of Hamelin until a bolder few started throwing stones. One hit me in the small of the back. I turned to shout at them. The children sprang for cover and after that followed at a more respectful distance, racing from one hiding place to the next when they judged the coast was clear. It became a sort of game between us, though from my side not a particularly pleasant one. My back still smarted from the blow.

I have to admit that I got myself lost. The stony passage-ways weave this way and that, the houses all look the same, their height blocking out any possible reference point, and, when I considered that after the next turn I should find myself back at the 'Aqil's house, where we were guests, I found I had walked up a blind alley.

Two women giggled at me before scuttling into a doorway. The children massed around the only point of egress. Their numbers had swelled. Some were really quite old and carried stones the size of small boulders. It had been wrong perhaps to shout at them.

The temperature had meanwhile dropped and with it a murkiness descended on the village like a London fog. A storm was clearly brewing, most exceptional for this time of year: I must return home, and quickly too.

The Gods looked kindly on me, for once. In answer to my prayers they sent a venerable old man dressed completely in white, a large white turban perched atop his head, who parted the children with his stick and walked up the alley, looking through me in the most peculiar way. He wasn't blind, or anything like that, he'd merely decided I wasn't there.

Smiling my thanks, I ran back the way I had come, and as I did so the wind rose swiftly and the rains began, sluicing from the heavens to form torrents on the ground that rushed through the alleyways. By the time I reached the house – which was closer than I had imagined – I looked as if I had taken a ducking and spent a miserable afternoon, my teeth clacking with cold, wrapped in a blanket as I watched the storm break around us. I wondered if Mr Fergusson were safe. Did he at that very moment struggle with Yūsuf back across the mountains, his path made treacherous by the storm?

Without him I feel lost again and try to hurry along the hours by imagining his route and how he might look with the rain beating down his face. It gives me a little comfort. A fear rises unbidden that he has turned his head in some other direction, now that he has broken free. With Mr Fergusson, one never knows for certain what he may do. I'll go to bed early and try to fill my empty hours with sleep.

———

9 January 1911

They came in the middle of the night, F. and Yūsuf who has adopted a most amusing swagger after the success of his journey up the Wādi Sihām. I should have been asleep; I wasn't. I tossed and turned on the floor, sick with worry and a shivering chill. My joy at having him back has been tempered by what I learn of his plans, but I tell myself that the dangers he chooses to court have nothing to do with me.

Yūsuf had many good stories to tell. I've given him his extra pay and requisitioned my mare with a few stern words: even the best of servants must learn to toe the line.

At Hodeidah he'd joined a merchant caravan bearing Manchester calico and other necessities of life up to Sanʿā. The local gendarmeries provided a mounted guard, courtesy of the Turks, who'll hop with rage when they discover whose stores they have so loyally protected. The guard notwithstanding, my man was shot at several times by lawless bandits looking for easy loot.

At Idz, as planned, he'd fallen sick, doubtless with much unnecessary drama, and withdrawn from the caravan. The other merchants would have been astonished to see the sick man rise from his bed and walk, no sooner had they passed out of sight. F. had already seen to the business of the mules – he'd hired a full two score – and after a short rest the two set out with a guide for their return to Hajarah. A band of Turkish footsoldiers chased them across a mountain, giving up only when the downpour began. One of the mules was lost down a precipice, taking with it some of my camp accoutrements but not my instruments, praise God, which I find in excellent condition.

After we'd found Yūsuf a space to sleep below stairs, F. and I discussed our plans. The British Museum is nothing but a front: I was right to question his suitability on that score. But what I hadn't suspected was that the 'business' he wishes to conclude in the interior is with the Imam himself. I wish he'd told me this before. Our joining forces makes no sense at all. His way lies to the north, to the rebel fortress at Shehārah, a dangerous journey at the best of times, while I am headed east. I asked him what his business concerned.

He didn't answer at once. He sat on the floor, wrapped in his blanket, staring out of the low windows into the night. I tried to read his mind, a closed book.

Eventually he looked me squarely in the face. 'I've got something for him,' he said. 'From the Sultan at Lahej.'

'What can the Sultan give him? And why send you?'

'There's money in it,' he replied matter-of-factly. 'A lot. I've sunk my savings in the deal. Do you know what that means? Four miserable years are riding on my back. Success is waiting for me now. I've worked for her damned hard and this time she'll not slip my grasp.'

'Impossible. We can't trade with our enemies.'

'The Imam quarrels with the Turks, not us.'

'What does Aden think?'

'I never asked. The Sultan at Lahej is thick as thieves with the General.'

'In that case . . . ' I remembered my conversations with Captain Kincaid at Aden. He certainly talked of the Sultan as chief among our friends in the Protectorate. But what would the Turks say? Although I don't mind annoying them a little this mission is of a different order altogether. Anyway, I thought, confused, my journey is to Māreb not the Imam at Shehārah.

'Come here,' he said, for we were sitting in our corners. I walked the room and sat beside him on the floor. He felt my face. The house was quiet. Only a distant sound of thunder. 'Will you come with me, Elinor?' he asked. 'It'll work out, I promise you.'

He used my name for the first time, spoken with a softness that urged me to throw good sense to the wind and follow

---

where he chose to lead. Those brimstony eyes, they're black as night. I'm out of my depth. I sought adventure, yes, but this . . . ? Already branded a spy, he now wishes to turn me into a collaborator. I couldn't refuse and couldn't tell him yes.

We went to our separate beds, undecided. I face another sleepless night, racked by the fear of losing him again. But what shall I do at Shehārah? I have no place in others' politics. With James by my side . . . It makes no sense to travel north; my journey has another purpose, to which I must stick firm. What would I tell them at home? I've met a man who's taken my fancy and we're off to join forces with the rebels? They'd conclude I'd lost my head when it's really my heart that needs attention. I've never known a man like James before. He turns my resolution to dust. I write what passed between us, that's all, and leave the rest unsaid.

Whatever I choose to do we must leave soon. The mountains are alive with menace. Each man gives off an air of expectancy, as we wait for the battles to begin.

10 January 1911

I fear we've left it too late; they're shooting up in the hills and Hajarah has declared against the Turk. The situation is abominably delicate. God knows how we can explain our presence here, to anyone.

I've tried to impress this on F. who refuses to take it seriously. We should lie low, he says, until the storm moves on. He fails to realize that we're sucked into the very eye of the storm and might provoke an international incident. I mean, the Turks and ourselves are meant to be friends, and here we are lodged among Turkish foe.

No, my friend, we can't simply lie low as you propose, though what we can do presently defeats me. We can't send a message to the Turks at Menākhah – no one would take it over for us; and if the Turks discovered the Imam's stores, we'd be marched to the coast in chains. Or shot. Nor can we thank our hosts and leave: the blast of gunshot echoes through these hills and I hear even now the heavy pounding of the guns at Menākhah. I never did like wars – they always succeed in messing up one's plans.

11 January 1911

Today I witnessed a sight more horrible than I have seen; it turned me sick at heart. They brought him straight to me, a gaggle of keening women whose shrieks and yells rose above the distant sounds of battle, and laid him at my feet, his blood draining away before my eyes to form a ruddy pool on the floor that grew in size until it lapped at my skirts. I recognized him instantly, one of the *'Aqil*'s sons, his leg shot away below the knee. The knee was bent, I remember that, and waggled in the air, its stump a squashy pulp from which protruded jagged bits of bone and dangled flesh. Horrible. Horrible.

A sort of greenness came over me. I sank to the floor or I would faint away. The women filled the room. Apart from myself only the lad was silent, his face drained grey by his approaching death. Great empty eyes implored me to save him but what could I do? I'm not a doctor. I couldn't dose him with salts and send him on his way.

Had F. not arrived at that moment, I don't know what we should have done. He cleared the room at once, despatched the women to the kitchens for boiling water, buckets of it, ordered me to search my bags for lint and antiseptic solution. Numb with shock, I watched him form a tourniquet from his pocket handkerchief, and always that stain of blood seeping outwards on the floor. Yūsuf hung about the doorway, eyes like saucers and his pigtails on end.

The boy soon died, of course. He gurgled like a babe and then . . . nothing. After a moment's silence, the wailing began afresh, a most inhuman din that shocked me by its absence of shame. My grief shall be a private thing, not this abandoned caterwauling.

After the boy's truncated remains had been carted away, F. came over to sit with me. I felt so womanly-weak when I had wanted to be strong, and tried to explain how I felt. But he was very gentle with me. 'Don't be too hard on yourself. It isn't easy at first. I'm used to wars,' he said, 'and revolution. You soon grow hard towards the sufferings of man.'

Putting his arm around my shoulders he rested my head on his breast. To my relief I cried and soon I slept, still held by those strong arms. I dreamed of green fields and of Maunton, and when I was woken by the sound of muffled wailing his worried face smiled down at me. He rarely smiles, does James, as if smiling gives the game away and there is little he shall give away for free.

This adventure has thrown us together for good or ill and even if we're an oddly-matched pair we shall continue our journey together toward our separate goals. I shall emerge a different person from the one who set out, full of hope, from Marseilles. I feel a change come over me and know that I gain in strength as my shortcomings are revealed. At times this frightens me. I wonder if anyone else will notice the difference. Will Father realize that his dear, sweet child is sweet no longer? That she's branded by the hardships she has shared and driven by a new hunger that seeks stronger meat than any she has known before. I have become another, that's the truth of it, and wonder where this journey will end.

12 January 1911

I must now go with F. to Shehārah. The mountains are too dangerous to proceed alone. Having thrown in my lot with him, I wish to see the business through and am relieved to have put a stop to my indecision.

Our presence in the village has become an embarrassment.

Although they dare not harm us, F. and the 'Aqil have exchanged rough words and the women, when not busy shrieking their heads off, look at me spitefully as if it's my fault their menfolk are expiring like fleas. Even Yūsuf has shed his swagger and sits disconsolately on the stairs, whittling at a stick from which he fashions strange, misshapen beasts.

According to the 'Aqil's intelligence, the fighting is concentrated around Menākhah and Turkish reinforcements have not yet come up from the coast. If we double back on our tracks and then head north around the Jebel Beni Ismā'īl we should escape the worst of it. We came as travellers and now must take like outlaws to the hills.

13 January 1911

Yūsuf and I spent the day sorting and re-sorting my stores of which I'm allowed to keep only the bare essentials: my beloved instruments, two changes of outfit, enough tins of food and hard biscuits to last a week, a roll of bedding to soften the stony rocks, the lightest of my camp furniture, rope, sacks, oil, candles and my medicine chest which contains quinine, camphorodyne, chinosol, Epsom salts, bandages, and boric lint. The rest we gave away to lighten our load and buy the 'Aqil's complaisance. I understand he was delighted with my glassware, and so he should be. F. did not take kindly to my suggestion (made in jest) that he should bequeath him the Imam's stores instead. In return for our gifts, my gifts, the 'Aqil has promised us a guide.

We discussed at length how we should dress. Arab clothes have the advantage of disguise but make us clear targets for the Turks. European clothes will draw attention from both sides but at least we'd be shot for ourselves. In the end, we opted for the latter. I'm pleased to look myself once more.

14 January 1911

Written in haste, to the west of the Jebel Beni Ismāʿīl. We're lucky to have escaped with our lives. I shall never again underestimate the difficulties of dealing with men who are obstinate, ignorant, greedy and disingenuous, all at the same time.

The ʿAqil came himself to open the gates for us at midnight. 'May your wisdom multiply,' he said to my companion, 'and may your seed scatter across the earth.' I didn't appreciate at the time that he meant it literally. The leave-takings done, he passed us over to the tender care of his guide, a squint-eyed fellow with a brigand's sense of humour who scampered on ahead, calling from time to time to indicate the route.

The slopes were blanketed in murky fog. We could see no more than a couple of yards before our noses. The night was cold as sin. Yūsuf, half-dead with fright, sang to calm his nerves, a frightful dirge: 'Allah, be with us always, Allah, guide and guard us'. F. swore at him to stop with a warning that he'd get us all shot. Yūsuf ignored him, preferring Turkish bullets to *jinn*. All the while the guide led us a most roundabout route from the village – at times we headed due east directly into the mouth of Menākhah's guns. And then, God rot his soul, he gave a last shout and disappeared.

So dark was the night, and so treacherous the way, we could neither advance nor retreat, and must sit out our impatience, enduring Yūsuf's nervous clatterings (I feared his teeth might drop out) as we waited for a first glimmer of light to reveal our whereabouts. It's just as well we did. When daybreak pierced at last the damp Scotch mist, we found ourselves perched on the brink of a truly awesome ravine.

We turned our beasts round, no easy matter in the circumstances, and headed back the way we had come. My map runs out north of Menākhah. From now we journey on our own, helped only by my compass and the stars.

15 January 1911

As F. so rightly said, one must harden one's heart towards the sufferings of man. Although the sights of this journey shall haunt me always, I've stopped my tears at man's barbarity to man.

Today we passed through one of the rebel villages down towards Khamīs Beni Sa'īd. Spindly columns of smoke rose into the air and vultures circled slowly overhead. It might have been a butcher's shop, staffed by novices. Bodies spewed about the ground, missing various limbs. A nasty, sickly-sweet stench that caught in one's throat. Doors to the squalid shops torn from their hinges, possessions trampled in the rush for loot.

An eerie silence hung like a pall above the sights of mindless destruction, a silence that betokened of the wrath of God, which shall be visited even unto the seventh generation. *The queen of the south shall rise up in the judgement with this generation, and shall condemn it* . . . Us too, I suppose. We're all tainted by history.

We ambled across the square, turning our beasts away from the worst of the carrion. In the tumbled ruins of a house, I spied a child, a girl, no more than a mite, really, whose sharp urchin face watched me with a look of accusation. In better times I would have stopped to help. But that was yesterday. Today I just rode on.

16 January 1911

This land is not for me, and what was once my goal has receded into the depths of the Empty Quarter. I doubt if I'll ever reach it now. Who cares? We ride, we stop, we eat, we fall into a pit-like sleep, we talk from time to time, we cross this bitter land as wraiths, unseeing and unseen, peering over our shoulders like Turks in case we're stabbed from behind. It's all the same to me.

———

Yesterday my companion shot and killed a Turk, a boy soldier, ragged and hungry, who popped up by the wayside waving his arms like a lunatic. F. reached for his gun. We all knew what would happen next. The boy knew. I knew. Yūsuf knew. F., of course, knew exactly what he was doing. No one prevented him. The boy looked up in surprise. Why me? he seemed to ask. It isn't fair. I never wanted to come. But F. stopped his cry with a bullet through the throat.

Later, after we'd forded the river and stopped to rest beneath an *'ilb* tree, I asked him why the boy must die. 'Don't be a fool,' he said. 'The boy could have given us away. You can't be sentimental about your enemies.'

'The Turks are my friends.'

'Then why do you creep about behind their backs? Is that the way to act with friends?'

He looked angry and is – I think – more sentimental about this killing business than he cares to admit. I lacked the strength to argue with him further. I slept and did not dream.

17 January 1911

We've passed up the *wādi*, praise God, and now approach a village which they say is called el-Mirwāh. The tribesmen here have sided with the Imam, and lent a guide to take us on to Shehārah, 'Ali by name, a distant cousin of the Sheikh of the Dhu Mohammed. He and Yūsuf have already fallen out over the matter of who is in charge.

Our route up the *wādi* afforded easy passage but the bare, stony rock-face on either side oppressed me terribly. I felt that we were watched at every step. That even the hills have eyes and that behind those craggy boulders crouched an army of men, ready to pick us off one by one at the hour of their choosing. Yūsuf gibbers to the trees – demons, he believes, and stops to pray whenever he finds a pile of stones by the wayside. One of the mules is lame. My mare refuses all food.

We form a sorry band, stumbling across this war-torn land like blinded beggars searching for a gold we cannot see.

18 January 1911

The danger of being shot at from all sides has mercifully receded and we may travel openly once more. The Turk, despised as a foreign interloper, has never made much inroad here. 'Ali brings us news at every halt. They say the Vali at San'ā has declared a state of siege and that the Porte has sent General 'Izzet Pasha to take command of military operations. Knowing the General's reputation of old, I hope that's true. Of all their commanders, he's the one most likely to knock some sense into rebel heads; Turkish ones too.

Already we resemble travellers again, having exchanged our tired mounts, my mare among them, for ones that are fresher in step. I was robbed over the deal as I was near Hajeilah and am a little perturbed that F. has ceased to reckon all the monies I disburse. When I broached the subject, as indirectly as possible, he flew into a sulk.

'Don't worry,' he said. 'You'll get back what I owe, and more.'

I don't care to be thought of as mean but, when I accepted to travel with him, my understanding was that we would be equal in all things, including the matter of expenses.

He has become a most tyrannical taskmaster. He roars at Yūsuf at the slightest provocation and becomes quite enraged whenever I sit apart from the others to compose this journal. My scribblings, he calls it with a sneer.

I wonder why he chose to travel with me. And why I remain so meekly in his party, when I could set myself free. I find myself hunting small ways to please him, showing him the best flowers and the birds, and waiting for his eyes to close in sleep before I sleep myself. Although such attentions clearly irk him further, I cannot help myself. His darkness has entrapped my will.

Poor Yūsuf slinks about the camp, tail between his legs, having decided that 'Ali wishes to poison him. 'Ali is, in fact, the best of fellows; without his impish good cheer, we'd sink into the swamp of our bickerings. I asked him how many forces the Imam could command. 'Outside his kingdom,' he replied, 'about 300,000. Inside, as many as the spreading locusts and the running flood.' From that I conclude he has more than half a dozen. A number, it seems, are hostages from neighbouring tribes, all boys, some as young as five, who are lodged in the dungeons at Hajjah to the north. It's a cruel land that enforces its promises through the suffering of infants. I wonder how my young nephews would respond to such barbarity.

I feel so far away from home. They must be worried sick as news of this revolt unfolds. Father will have doubtless contacted the Foreign Office who may have heard already, from Wendell via Aden, that disregarding official 'advice' I have made my way into the interior. It's too late now to wish I'd stayed at home. Father will understand that this journey means more to me than playing by the rules. Or rather, that it did once. What it means now I cannot say.

19 January 1911

A scare earlier today has put us back on our guard. Having dipped into the Wādi Sharas, between Hajjah and Kuhlān, we were resting in a flat hollow ringed with euphorbia trees when the most frightful din erupted and we found ourselves besieged by a wild band of gun-toting tribesmen who roared around us on their ponies, shooting into the air and shrieking in unison. There's nothing much one can do in such circumstances except to sit tight and hope they're pretty poor shots. Yūsuf tried to dig himself a hole in the ground, much to 'Ali's scorn. F. kept his head admirably, accepting such behaviour as perfectly normal in the wilds.

After a few minutes, during which time the guns were pointed ever more closely at our heads and we felt the bullets whizzing past our ears, F. conferred with 'Ali (he doesn't talk to me) then walked slowly over towards his stores. Forcing the lid of one of the boxes, he drew out several rifles, all, from what I could see, in mint condition. The tribesmen – four in number though they made enough noise for seventeen – slipped off their ponies in mid-gallop and came to inspect the booty. They asked if F. could give them the proper ammunition. This caused no problem. He simply went over to one of the other boxes and took out cartridges by the armful.

I have a horrible feeling I know what this means and that F. is not what he seems. I tried to convince myself that what he carries in his bags is a matter for him and his conscience, not mine. My reticence took him by surprise. As we continued our journey, riding – most unusually – side by side, he dropped needling remarks like, 'They seem to prefer Winchesters to French Le Gras.' I ducked the conversation as best I could and sat by myself as soon as we halted at dusk.

20 January 1911

For the first time we did not break camp today. F. went off with 'Ali as soon as the mist cleared, saying the day was perfect for sport. They had spent much of the night whispering and laughing near my bed. I would have joined them if anyone had asked.

The day stretched blankly ahead. One gets accustomed to a journey's ordered monotony: to break one's habits is to risk the temptation of idle hands. I attended to some light mending, read a little Herodotus, then went for a walk up the steep slopes on the eastern edge of the valley pursued by Yūsuf who hoped I might save him from the *jinn* of our campsite, a perfectly ordinary spot though hotter than a baker's oven because of our drop in altitude.

I must have seen too much because this landscape strikes me as tame, the jagged mountains merely more of the same, the terraces only mildly spectacular, lacking the neat husbandry of those around Menākhah.

Back at camp, no sign of the others. I slept a while, then sat on a rock to wait for their return. They rounded the spur as the sun sank behind the hills, F. and 'Ali on foot, followed by two horsemen bearing guns. I thought for a wild moment that my friends had been captured, but no, the strangers dismounted and came into our camp where F. strutted about, giving orders for the reception of our guests. Yūsuf was sent for blankets and my shawl while I was told to build a fire of brushwood, quickly done in spite of the protests I wished to voice.

The flames jumped high as soon as the wood was lit and 'Ali took charge of the food, a couple of brace of rock pigeons, plucked and roasted over the fire which crackled and smoked, emitting an odour of the wilds that recalled, for me, my other journeys undertaken in happier circumstances. I kept to the shadows and watched.

The newcomers were fed first. They looked unsavoury fellows wrapped in their sheepskins, guns held ready by their sides. F. served them himself, attending to their every need in ways he never has to mine.

He's wild-looking enough but that night there was something demonic about him; I caught an unmistakable whiff of sulphur. It must have been the dark, the dancing flames; he looked to me a son of Lucifer. I wanted there and then to flee, take up my bed and run into the hills, anywhere that I might shake off the blackness in my heart. My feet refused to move.

Yūsuf stepped towards the fire, alerting the others to my presence. F. looked round and, when he saw me, gave a sort of smile, no, not a smile, that's too ordinary a word to describe his infamous expression. A wicked leer. He motioned me forwards. I stepped into the fire's heat and met the lustful stares of the strangers. They had a certain cut-throat charm, being younger than I had assumed, beardless, each with a raffish air that I found oddly reassuring. One grinned, the other curled his lip.

F. bid me stand by the flames, like a slave girl under the hammer, while he enunciated my charms. The others laughed. It was monstrous, really. He called me his second-best wife.

Yūsuf was right about the spirits of this place, as evil a bunch as one could ever hope to encounter. Before they left, they danced for us, those wild men, flashing their daggers in the firelight as they jigged from foot to foot, while 'Ali beat the drums, or rather, not for me they danced, a mere woman. They danced for Mr Fergusson.

21 January 1911

We've reached the parting of ways. F. and 'Ali continue to Shehārah while Yūsuf and I head east to Khamir. All is for the best: we couldn't continue as before, nor could we change our ways, and I accept our parting with a spirit approaching equanimity.

We've quarrelled, of course, over the matter of the Imam's stores and heaven knows what besides, a quarrel that dogged our heels from the moment we woke, F. nursing a foul head (if he drank, it was after the others had gone), myself a sort of emptiness, drained by those devilish revellings of yesterday.

He drove us hard throughout this last, dreadful day, first due north along the Wādi Sharas, then north-east towards Hūth, speaking only to chide, and shout at Yūsuf who continues to complain.

We were all relieved when he gave the word to set up camp beside a native well, a dreary spot scattered with black basalt rocks. Yūsuf busied himself about our meal, the usual fare: unleavened bread donated by a villager, a pot of boiled fowl, and a boiled egg each. To give myself something to do, I asked 'Ali if I could sketch him by the well, hoping to enliven my composition with his wild looks and heathen attire.

That was my mistake. Not that 'Ali objected, but Mr Fergusson did. Looking back now I realize that any spark would have ignited our quarrel because he was looking for a pretext to have done with me. Although it hurts to write this, I'm sure it's true.

I had nearly finished my sketch – and was moderately pleased with its success – when F. stormed over and shouted at 'Ali for loitering like a lazy dog. The mules needed fodder. He was damned if he would see to them himself. (That is the gist of it, anyway.) 'Ali jumped to his feet but I couldn't resist the temptation to offer a mild rebuke. 'Ali's 'laziness' was my bidding entirely.

At this, my erstwhile friend threw the book at me. He called me pampered, self-obsessed, a dilettante, stupid, arrogant, unutterably silly, and something of a bore. There were other things, too, but those were the gibes that hurt. I took it bravely on the chin, saying that when one travels one loses all sense of proportion, and that after a decent supper he'd feel himself again. My response served only to provoke him further; he positively stamped with rage and so I enquired calmly if he suffered from the sun. That did it, I'm afraid. A sort of polar cold descended on us. He looked at me with icy eyes.

'You think me mad, Miss Grace? Perhaps I'll run amok. Does that frighten you?'

'Not in the least. I think you're under stress. We all are.'

He looked for a second as if he wanted to strangle me. 'You know what I'm doing, don't you?'

'Possibly.' I backed away.

'I'm taking guns to the Imam at Shehārah.'

'Why tell me this now?'

'We're running guns, Miss Grace, you and I. If caught, we'd be shot on sight, and no one would lift a finger in our defence. Why else should I sneak in by the back door? The mailship, remember. I could hardly show this lot to the Turks and hope to get away with it. You must have known.'

'Perhaps I did suspect . . . I mean, it didn't make sense. But now . . . I can't continue after this. I'll have to leave at once.'

'I thought you wanted adventures. You'd get some with me, to be sure.'

'They're not exactly the ones I had in mind.'

His laugh was like the cackling of a jackal. I felt the spit on my face. He really was quite mad by now. Over his shoulder I glimpsed Yūsuf watching us, open-mouthed. He must have heard the shouting. I asked F. to calm down as his behaviour was unseemly in front of the servants. He turned and roared at Yūsuf who looked at him in shock then ran away.

'So you'll not come with me? I didn't think you would. Doesn't square with your conscience, I suppose.'

'I told you before, I don't believe in trading with our enemies.'

'I'm backing the future, Miss Grace, not the past.'

'I side with my Government, and yours.'

'You damned well would. You haven't the vision to see for yourself. Your *Government* always hedges its bets and then, at the last possible minute, shoves the lot on the wrong horse.'

'I'll have you know your sentiments are treasonous.'

'Take them as you please. I've had enough.'

'Enough of what, Mr Fergusson?'

Like a couple of bull terriers we glared at one another. I try to remember exactly how he looked. I'm sure it's important but the image refuses to hold. He waved his hand in answer to my question, a wave that might have signified me, this cruel land, even the business of running guns to Shehārah, most likely all three, but was he really tired of me or did he wish to turn me away for my own good?

The rift was plainly permanent. I knew that in his present state there was nothing for it but to accept defeat as gracefully as one could. I held out my hand. He looked aghast and then his whole body shook with raucous laughter, a shockingly raw sound from a civilized man. Wiping away the tears, he took my hand most forcefully. 'Good for you, Elinor,' I heard him say beneath his breath.

Feeling quite sick inside, I followed him back to camp, sad that our last walk together should be so strained. A hoopoe bird flitted among the dusty scrub. I pointed it out to him, and told him how the hoopoe had been the first to tell Solomon about Sheba. He knew the story from the *Qur'ān*, even quoted some of it, to my surprise.

This gave me heart to ask a question that had troubled me often as we lay under the stars. I asked him why he'd ever wanted to travel with me. The approach at Aden was his, I reminded him. I hadn't asked to come.

He looked to neither right nor left. He probably hadn't seen the hoopoe. Not all are natural ornithologists. At last he stopped and turned on me impatiently. 'You're always the same,' he said, 'wanting explanations. Can't you accept that a man might decide to do something because it pleases him? I was bored, that's all. I thought it might work out. You had a rum reputation in the *sūqs*. I wanted company. God knows, one gets one's fill of travelling alone.'

'What sort of reputation?' I asked indignantly.

'I thought you'd got some fire in your belly. Take that as my excuse. I was wrong, Miss Grace, just wrong. I needed money, dammit. Now do you understand?'

'You could have asked. I would have lent you some gladly, if you'd acted decently.'

'I'll not be beholden to anyone.'

'You took it, just the same.'

'I got you here; isn't that enough in exchange? It was as honest a way as I could think of. Here . . . ' He pulled a bag of

Maria Theresa dollars from his waistcoat. 'Take what you're owed. Take the lot, if you like. There's more coming.'

'Where did you get it? Those men, did they give it you? They came from the Imam, didn't they?'

He threw the coins at my feet.

'That money's for the guns, isn't it? I'll not have Turkish blood on my hands.'

'I don't care whose blood,' he said, 'as long as they pay well enough.'

'Keep it,' I said and picking up my skirts I left his coins in the dirt and returned to camp.

We ate Yūsuf's boiled fowl in silence, his harsh words sitting at table like unwelcome guests. Already a line had divided us, with Yūsuf and myself on one side, 'Ali and Mr Fergusson on the other.

When the meal was cleared away and our stores sorted for the morning's ride I went off by myself to regain some measure of strength. The days have taken their toll and I wondered if I had any reserves left for the great journey ahead.

The constellations stretched across the sky, brightest among them Sirius, the dog star, close on the heels of the hunter, Orion. The night was vibrant with their flickerings. One cannot feel quite alone, under such a heaven, and I regained some of my former optimism. In spite of all that has happened, I am convinced that this journey shall be the making of me.

Hearing a noise in the scrub I turned and saw a man crouching in the sand. Although his face was hidden I knew that F. had come to say goodbye. He didn't say much; he certainly didn't apologize, that's not his way. But he gave me a letter he carries from the Imam at Shehārah, a form of safe conduct and by-his-leave that bears his very regal seal.

'You'll need it,' he said. 'The tribes out east, the Ahl el-Mashriq, are damnably fierce.'

'Don't you want it yourself?'

'I'm almost there, Elinor. Tomorrow I'll be among friends.'

We walked slowly back to camp. Conscious of him by my side, I wished that he would take me in his arms, just once, and I would carry the memory of that embrace into the central plains and down into the Empty Quarter. It wasn't much to ask but the words stuck in my throat and I was too shy to take the lead.

We came to my bedroll. He put his hands on my shoulders and leaned against me. That was the closest we got. As he turned away I remembered the book I'd bought in his stead at Hodeidah, the copy of the *Qur'ān*. I told him to wait, as this was the time for gifts. I found it again after fumbling in my bags.

He took it awkwardly. 'There was a school . . . ' he said. 'I taught the native boys in Harar. This was the only text they knew. Thank you, Miss Grace. It's very kind.'

He walked into the night. I stopped myself running after him. It's no use now. We've reached the parting of ways.

I'll learn to laugh at our disagreement, which was truly for the best because in any expedition there can be only one person in charge. From tomorrow, *in-shallah*, that person shall be me.

★

22 January 1911   *Hajjah district*

Dear Wendell,

It was damned good of you to help us. I'll be for ever in your debt. Miss Grace will too. She's asked me to say that she hopes her sudden flight was never lain at your door.

You've probably heard the news that fighting broke out at Menākhah on or around January 8. We holed up for a time in one of the villages nearby and had the devil of a job breaking free. But here we are some way north of Hajjah, safe and well and even managing to get some sport. Next time you come up country, you should make your way over here where I can guarantee a good few days' entertainment.

I must, however, throw myself once more on your good will. It concerns Miss Grace who's decided, against all odds, to continue alone to Māreb. Although she's pretty resourceful, as you well know, I'm amazed at her foolhardiness, especially as the Sheikh at Māreb is notoriously fickle, coquetting now with the Imam, now with the Turk, so she'll not know which side to catch him on. I've done what I could to turn her away from the whole idea and got nowhere. But I worry about her, even so.

The favour I want to ask of you is this. Her journey to Māreb should last two, maybe three weeks. She's got some pretty tough country ahead of her and a whole configuration of warring tribes. Can you keep your ears to the ground for any hint of trouble and send out a search party if the situation deteriorates? Depending on the lie of the land, you may need to call on the Turks who'll be more than pleased to lay their hands on her. It's not an ideal solution but the best I can think of in the circumstances. I've also told her she should get in touch with you if the business turns sour.

Sorry to trouble you like this. I'm travelling north and

can't give her an address to contact me. I know you'll do your best.

Just one more thing. I'm always scrounging favours, aren't I? If anything happens to me, you know the sort of thing I mean, can you drop word to my sister Isobel Fergusson? She lives at 7 Maryhill Road, Glasgow. Tell her what you know, as gently as you can, and say that if she ever hears bad of me she must remember that everything I did, I did for her and Caroline. Caroline's my daughter, the sweetest, cleverest thing you ever saw. She was two when I left so I haven't been much of a father to her but by God I shall be, if given half a chance. You could also tell Isobel that you met me and that I seemed in good heart. I leave it up to you. But please don't mention Elinor. There's a whole history I can't explain. I hope it'll not come to that.

Please convey my warmest regards to Mrs Wendell, and young Lizzie. She's a fine girl, and must make her father very proud.

Your grateful friend,
James Fergusson

Part Two

SHEBA'S LAND

The heat rises off the sands. It hits me in the face, blinding in its sharp white light. Yūsuf thinks me mad. He watches me kick off my boots and drop to my knees like a pilgrim, skin scorched by the sands. And yet I do not flinch. How strange it feels to claim an inheritance one has never seen.

I've reached my goal at last. *A fine country and a gracious Lord* . . . Already the journey has slipped between the folds of my memory along with F. and all the rest. Did we really quarrel, or was that just a dream?

I thought of him often as we passed beyond the central highlands into the great peopled plains, moving ever eastwards towards our goal, barely sleeping, always on the move, a couple of tinkers beneath an empty sky. And if they watched us from afar they let us pass unchallenged, guessing correctly that we posed no threat, that tinkers are the least offensive of God's humble creatures. Then, as we started our long descent down the eastern escarpment, a stony land indeed, I looked into the blue shimmered haze and thought: Yes, my journey has been worth the candle, and all the loneliness endured these many days.

A sandstorm caught us as we neared our goal, Yūsuf and I. It tore along the valley so fiercely I feared a living death within its shifting dunes. We must dismount and crouch behind our mules, our bodies scourged by gritty sand, sharp as a whiplash. And when the wind moved on we walked like blacked-up niggers of the night out towards Māreb, capital of ancient

Saba, renowned through all Arabia for its stupendous fertility.

Saba had for a sign in their dwelling place two gardens, on the right and the left. Eat therefore of the provision of your Lord, and render thanks unto Him: a fine country and a gracious Lord. Now all is wretched, washed away by floods, the great dam burst, the wonder of the ancient world destroyed. The *Qur'ān* speaks of it to me, of the fruits of pride and of infidelity. *Yet they rebelled, and We sent unto them the flood of el-'Arim; and We transformed their two gardens into two plots full of bitter herbs and tamarisks, and a few jujube trees. Such was our punishment of their infidelity. Do We punish other than the unfaithful?* This land shall now be mine, my dwelling place.

Through all the time we journeyed I never wrote a word, hoarding my pennies of strength to keep my face turned east. Now the old habits return. Without a record of my daily tasks this journey shall be lost to posterity. And yet it seems an unnatural act to squeeze the ragged edges of events into the neat compartments of a journal. My days run into each other. The sun and moon change places in accordance with their own calendars, not mine, and I have anyway lost count of the date. Is it really twenty-one days since we parted? Or is it twenty-three? I can't see it matters very much.

Yūsuf says we must pay our respects at once to the Sharif at Māreb whose permission we need to live here undisturbed. I'll do it gladly if it brings him peace of mind. It may already be too late. He tells me that three horsemen approach from the direction of the old village which lies back upon a mound, crenellated like a medieval fortress. To judge from the clouds of dust, the men are travelling at speed.

The Sharif wants money, of course. God, how I detest their boundless rapacity. I said I'd pay him by the week, planning thus to eke out his complaisance.

As Arabs go, he's one of the worst, a scraggy man with thin

06/04/91 16:30   E   7   2024
NO REFUNDS, EXCHANGES ONLY
WITHIN 7 DAYS WITH A RECEIPT

PUBLISHER PRICE			CROWN SAVINGS	CROWN PRICE
1@	5.95	FIFTH PROFES	10%	5.36
1@	5.95	WHITE NINJA	10%	5.36
1@	5.99	SEA LION	10%	5.39
1@	5.95	GULF	10%	5.36
1@	20.00	PATRIOTS	20%	16.00
1@	65.00	AFRICAN ART	20%	52.00

SUBTOTAL	$	89.47
TAX @ 4.50%	$	4.03
TOTAL	$	93.50
TENDERED Check	$	93.50

CROWN SAVINGS $ 19.37

shanks, a light complexion and small, unhealthy eyes. From the way he glanced at the Imam's letter I suspect he's illiterate, although he clearly recognized the seal as genuine. As he doesn't care overmuch for the Imam the letter may anyway have harmed my case. I'll stay out of his way as much as possible and have refused his offer of an empty house in the village for which he required additional 'compensation'.

To this has Saba's glory descended. The village is anyway damnably hot, the only points in its favour being a handful of Sabaean stones, pilfered from the ruins, and a heat-hazed view across the *wādi* that would encompass my beloved ruins if only one had eyes to see.

We've set up camp near some settled Bedu by a well, a truly primitive folk. The men wear calico loincloths held up by leather belts and redouble their ferocity by smearing a mixture of sesame oil and indigo across their naked torsos. The women are more decently covered in long, shapeless shifts. Both sexes deck themselves with much silver jewellery and carry a cornelian amulet said to cure a snake bite by its touch. I hope it's never put to the test.

The Bedu helped us to erect a small, goathair tent, a very rough and ready affair, and shelter for the animals. As Yūsuf is out of his depth I must see myself to the business of securing provisions. We live off *'asid*, a sort of millet porridge; dried berries of the *'ilb* tree; camel's milk, when we can get it; and a leaden bread baked on the ashes of their *abal* fires.

Yūsuf has, I'm afraid, succumbed to a gloomy state of mind and asks leave to return home. I've given him my blessing, knowing full well that he's far too unheroic to undertake the journey alone. He sits in my tent drawing faces in the sand and uttering doom-ridden prophecies that wash above my head.

For company I've adopted two children of the desert (they really adopted me), Hamid and Mahmūd, who come with me each day to the ruins where they squat in the burning sand, watching me with quiet fascination. Mahmūd, the older of the two, is sadly boss-eyed. He wears a loincloth of goatskin and carries a sacred stick which he waves whenever I come too close. Hamid, my favourite, runs like the wind, quickly outstripping his taller companion, and has a jocular expression akin to that of a monkey. Both have curiously shaved heads, a strip of hair across the crown, some tufts above the forehead, the rest shorn.

They disappear at night to sleep God knows where, leaving me troubled by my demons of the past, by faces and remembered imaginings of things that cannot be. F. comes to me then in dreams, and sometimes when I wake. He's twice asked forgiveness for his cruel words, the day our quarrel broke. I've said my forgiveness is his for the asking. But sometimes he's unkind, scowling with a buzzard's eye, and then I toss and turn in the cold, impatient for the soft grey light of dawn, and the fierce sun that banishes all dreamings of the day.

I've entered into lengthy negotiations with the Sharif for an army of men to start my excavations. One site interests me especially. They call it Mahram Bilqīs, a temple of refuge so sacred that all who step within its hallowed walls are free, from kings to the most wretched of criminals. As far as archaeological sites are concerned, it lacks the glories of Palmyra and Petra's awesome majesty, and yet its limestone shafts reaching like fingers through the sand have thrilled me more than words can ever say.

I must attempt to describe it properly. The site is surrounded by an oval wall some thirty feet high and twelve feet across at the base, its inner curve buried under a mound of sand. The carefully cut stones, one or two of which I have revealed using my bare hands, measure about five feet in length. Leading off from this enclosure is the temple proper, a hall of oblong pillars of Jurassic limestone, maybe thirty feet in height (as they poke up through the sands it's impossible to be more precise), each topped with a small cubic elevation to which the roof structure must have been attached. The pillars at either side, three or four in number, are shorter, as are the seven remaining pillars at the near side, one of which leans precariously against the next. The actual entrance from the ovoid enclosure is marked by two squat cairn-like structures built of stones. That is all. The rest lies underneath.

It should be seen at evening when geometric shadows creep across the rippled sands, pointing outwards to the desert's unimaginable emptiness. I sit there often with my two desert waifs, enthralled by the sun's last glow, knowing that soon I must stir myself to excavate her secrets and that one can't return empty-handed from a journey such as mine, and yet . . . I hesitate to write this, Mr Mills and all the rest would think me mad, but I feel most strongly that to dig within this sacred place is tantamount to sacrilege, that what was buried should remain for ever so.

I can't imagine what has come over me. I am, after all, an archaeologist and archaeologists are expected to dig. Perhaps tomorrow I'll feel myself again and can set about the business with renewed energy. At present, I treat my negotiations with the Sharif as an idle game. He throws in impossible demands which I counter with idiotic stipulations of my own, the whole a parody of how not to proceed.

We are no longer alone at the ruins; a fourth has joined our vigil. So far he's neglected to identify himself. He sits up to the right where the wall joins the hall of pillars, clutching an ancient rifle which he points to the sky. I call him Michael as he has a touch of the archangel about him. He made the boys a little nervous at first but now we're accustomed to his presence and I invite him to share our midday bread, which he accepts without a word of thanks as if it were his due.

The Sharif has demanded that his men be allowed to pray five times a day – such prayer times to be included in their paid work – and that they must be fed, at my expense, in the village. With all that toing and froing I estimate I'll get some three hours' work per man per day which is hardly sufficient to dig a sand-castle. I've therefore increased the number of required workers from twelve to twenty-two, plus twice as many boys, and said they can share the original wages between them. Not surprisingly, the Sharif refused and we're back exactly where we started, which is nowhere.

As the negotiations drag on I gave myself the day off to visit the site of the ancient dam, a journey some two hours west at the entrance of the Wādi Shibwān. My 'family' accompanied me, Yūsuf included, and what a strange band we must have looked to any casual observer. At the head of the procession I rode my mule flanked by Hamid and Mahmūd who ran the whole distance barefoot in the sand. Yūsuf, whose mule carried our provisions and enough water for all, followed more slowly, shaking off his gloom to take at least a little interest in his surroundings. The archangel Michael brought up the rear, his rifle strapped to his back, half running, half walking, more of a lollop than a stride.

The valley is flat and wide, dotted with low stone structures that look like graves but are in fact remnants of Māreb's irrigation system. And all around are clumps of thorny 'ilb trees, the wild jujube, *Zizyphus spina-Christi*, and tamarisks flattened by the wind.

The site is truly one of the wonders of the ancient world. Most of the dam has gone but two great sluice gates remain, nearly a mile apart, which gives some idea of the structure's enormity. We visited the northern gate first where I took a rubbing of a perfectly preserved Sabaean inscription, pleased to set to work again. I shall return later for a more professional moulding. The dam holds nothing sacred for me.

Once we had walked around the battlements, where I was able to interest Yūsuf in the finer points of their construction, we made our way along a steep gulley to the southern sluice gate which, though smaller, is the better preserved of the two.

What joys awaited us there. A fair-sized river flowed beneath its base, coolly green in the midst of such aridity. I sent the others away and stepped fully clothed into its swift waters, shockingly cool, shallow at the edge then shelving steeply into the main channel. I let the current take me past the rocks towards my companions who bathed downstream, except for Michael who squatted on a rock, clutching his rifle as he does at the ruins. I'm sure he's sent to guard us, not to harm. I splashed with the boys in the shallows, my clothes hanging limply to my body, and then we spread ourselves to dry on the rocks under Michael's benevolent eye.

Our return to camp in the later afternoon was less felicitous. Someone had rifled my things. I've lost my field glasses, a ·32 Browning and all its ammunition, a mirror, my Herodotus, and some bandages from my medicine chest. I expect the Sharif had his hand in this as he's coveted my glasses for some time. I'll miss them, and my gun, and most of all the Herodotus, a gift from Father, which has been a very good companion.

By my rather shaky calculations I reckon that today is 21 February. Has a whole month passed since the parting of our ways? I eat little and sleep less and somehow thrive on my privations under the heartless sun which clamps upon me like a helmet.

My life is circumscribed. I rise at dawn to breakfast frugally and then as soon as Hamid and Mahmūd make their appearance we set off for the ruins where I take some elevations or scrape away the sand or simply sit and stare into the Empty

Quarter, waiting for Michael who appears each day when the sun has climbed halfway up the sky. I can't think how the rest of the day passes but it does, and towards evening I and my boys return home, sometimes calling at the throne of Bilqīs, Arsh Bilqīs, a line of five symmetrical pillars set close together in the sand, a sixth one broken off near the base. We don't care for these ruins half so much as for our own.

The sooner I hire myself some protection the better. I was woken in the night by rustling sounds within my tent. A lumpish shape against the entrance, a man, not Yūsuf, bent over my clothes. I saw his legs close to my bed, his bare feet, a fringe of kilt around his knees. I screamed. He dropped what he was holding (my lamp, unlit) and fled the tent, leaving me to cower in darkness, frightened to light the lantern as its oil had spilt and I might cause a conflagration. This time nothing was lost.

I called to Yūsuf who came, eventually, surly with sleep and not the least bit penitent for having wandered off into the night to find himself a more comfortable spot. I posted him at the entrance and passed a sleepless night, imagining each sound a new visitation. I think the man was sent to scare me away, but from what? If only F. were here to protect me. But he isn't. His business means more to him than I do. He doesn't care what happens to me. He's thrown me to the desert wolves and left me to fend for myself.

My negotiations with the Sharif have entered their final stage. He's dropped his requirement that the men should feed at the village while I've increased their wages to the proper amount. Yesterday they were marshalled for my inspection at the foot of the village (the boys I'll take as they come): twenty-four

sorry specimens standing raggedly to attention, the blind, the
lame, the wretched of the earth, the very sick, from whom I
must fashion a team of Herculean labourers. I refused to let
their obvious unsuitability discourage me. One's dreams do
not come easily on this good earth. The Sharif remained on
horseback throughout this ridiculous ceremony, riding up and
down the line in poor imitation of a general. I looked each man
in the eye and decided he must do.

My first task was to arrange the election of a foreman. When
they understood what I wanted, they clumped together and,
after much shouting and clearing of throats, thrust forward the
blackest ruffian, Sālih ibn Sēlim, who lacks three fingers from
one hand but is otherwise intact. In an odd sort of way I am
content with their choice as I prefer to deal directly with the
chief troublemaker who may otherwise foment discord behind my back. The Sharif and I shook hands on the deal: work
starts in three days' time.

He's come back to me at last. I always knew he would. That
when we said goodbye before Shehārah, it wasn't really
goodbye, just a necessary separation. I saw the puffs of dust
approaching from the west as I breakfasted at dawn. Even with
the naked eye, at such a distance, I knew it was he, that he
would never forsake me beneath these heathen skies.

Yūsuf was with me at the time and understood at once. I sat
and watched the dust grow larger as the distance shrank, aware
of my quiet happiness and Yūsuf fussing by my side. I would
have liked to prepare myself for him, to change my clothes and
wash my face and greet him in the best of circumstance. I sat
where I was and sent the boys away when they came. This day
was not for ruins, I told them. Michael too must wait.

He took a full two hours to reach my camp, this speck of
dust moving towards me across the plains, and as time leng-
thened I grew alarmed that he should take so long. All was

explained when he finally rode into camp, leading two miserable pack animals laden with stores. He fell from his mule half-dead into my waiting arms. His face was bruised and blood-caked. One arm hung limply by his side, the other hand was raw. He looked like a scarecrow, too tattered to scare the tiniest bird.

Holding his better arm about my shoulders I found strength to drag him to my tent where I laid him out on my bed and gently tore away his clothes. His body was covered in filthy cuts and sores and smelt abominably. He was thankfully too overcome to offer any resistance as I can't strip a man naked and fight him at the same time. I hope, when he recovers, he'll feel no shame. Yūsuf and I patched him up as best we could so that my tent soon resembled a battlefield.

I gave him water to drink, propping his head in my arms, and let him sleep, fanning his poor wounded face to keep away the flies which, scenting blood, swarmed out of nowhere to settle on his eyes and nostrils and the cuts on his skin. The tent grew mightily hot and I wondered if we shouldn't move into the village where I could tend far better to his needs. The desert is no place for a wounded man. We've plenty of time ahead of us to think of such things. What matters to me now is his return.

In the drowsy mid-afternoon, when even the flies were banished by the heat, he opened his eyes and looked about him in surprise. 'Is that you?' he asked. I'm sure he called my name. I told him not to speak, the better to conserve his energies. And so he slept some more as evening passed into night and I listened to the sounds of the desert and the Bedu encampment nearby, quitting my friend only once to contemplate the stars.

The Sharif has again put off the start of my excavations, claiming that the moment is not propitious (when will it ever be?). The spirits, he says, require more loot if I'm to win them over to my side. I remarked that the spirits hereabouts have clearly modelled themselves on the inhabitants, but was pleased nonetheless because this further delay allows me to devote all my attentions to F. who grows steadily stronger. I've given him my tent and sleep in snatches outside. He should be proud of me but isn't conscious long enough to know.

The sick are like infants in their terrible helplessness. They sleep, they wake to mew and whimper and seek the comfort of soothing words. I feel the roughness of his unshaven chin and ache to fold him in my arms.

The boys are with us constantly. Hamid in particular has proved himself a willing helper in the sick room. I've put him in charge of personal attentions, his hands as sure and skilled as any physician's. Mahmūd has also made himself useful tearing up endless petticoats to dress the wounds. F. likes to have them in the tent; he sleeps more easily when they are close at hand, and whispers to them sometimes in fevered speech. Yūsuf maintains the patient should be cupped. As if he hasn't suffered and bled enough already.

When the time comes, I'll ask him what happened at Shehārah, and whether he sold the rest of his stores.

F. is on the mend. He sat up yesterday as I dozed beside him on the ground. 'Elinor,' he said, 'I'm hungry as a lion.' I nearly wept for joy. Mahmūd fetched him goat's milk from the Bedu, and Yūsuf cooked him a stew. He ate with relish and afterwards slept soundly so I hope and pray the dangers have passed.

In the evening he asked to be carried outside where we sat like man and wife who gladly seek each other's company. Pain has etched its lines across his face. He looks much older than his forty years. I like him just as well as he is.

He'll not yet say what happened at Shehārah. I gather the

money has gone and he's a poorer man by far than when he came to these lands, having squandered his pride.

'They'll not have me beat,' he said, shaking his fist like the brave boy who thinks he has the measure of a dragon. I longed to draw him to me and show him in the only way I know that something has been gained in the end. I've money enough for both of us and shan't count the cost. He'll not have that to taunt me with again.

Later, when F. was put to bed, I rode over to the ruins. The moon rose high and round above my head, its gentle smile angled at a slant. As I stepped into the temple's ghostly shadows I felt a rush of exultation harsher than the wind, more terrible than the flood which sweeps across the land, cleansing, wiping out, obliterating the last blot of human imperfection to restore a terrible cold purity on which we may build the world anew.

The crash of waves ringing in my ears, I sank to my knees. A voice, a woman's voice, called to me from deep underground. *She came from the ends of the earth to hear the wisdom of Solomon; and behold, a greater than Solomon is here.* What does she want of me? Why has she beckoned me here across the mountains into her desert wastes?

I felt the wind subside and with it the flood receded into the night, discarding me like jetsam above the tide-mark. My time has not yet come. What does she mean, to play with me like this? She walked here once, a queen. 'Speak to me,' I shouted to the vanishing wind. 'What do you want?'

The temple held me in its net of silence. There was no answer. What should I expect? But, as I knelt among the spectral ruins, my exultation drained, I was startled to see a rock (I had presumed) take human form; it was the ever-faithful Michael who had guarded the temple night and day, patiently awaiting my return. I waved. He raised his rifle in salute then bounded off across the moonlit sands.

Now that F. gains strength I'm forced to alter my plans. He wants to set up house in the village, claiming that these desert fringes are far too vulnerable to attack. He trusts the Sharif less than I do, which isn't much, and his experiences at Shehārah have soured his view of humankind.

'Ali, it seems, is dead. I mourn his busy good humour and look again at the portrait I made of him *en route*, the portrait that cast us apart. Though I'm unskilled at likenesses and the work is barely complete, I've caught his impish smile. I'll keep the knowledge of his death from Yūsuf who may otherwise be tempted to gloat.

I'll miss my little camp in the desert and fervently wish – but this is nonsense – that I had the strength of will to resist.

The Imam took the guns and when it came to payment laughed in my friend's face, claiming the guns were a gift, long overdue, from the British Government. F. swore he was a merchant, not an emissary.

'In that case,' said the wily Imam, 'you'll claim your fees from them,' and duly wrote out a receipt in which he itemized the arms and ammunition he had received from the hands of a British subject, one James Nathaniel Fergusson.

What happened next I haven't ascertained. My friend says darkly that the Arab sells his soul for a mess of pottage and yours along with it. They get no more than they deserve. There is a dark side to his character that frightens me; a loneliness far wider than the empty spaces in which we live. I hear his cry for help, shrill as a bat's, and fear for him most dreadfully.

It's all arranged. We're to move to the village tomorrow, as paying guests of one of the shabby notables who owns an empty house by the walls.

Having heard of my friend's arrival, the Sharif paid us a visit accompanied by several armed men. F. had me show him to the tent from which I was then excluded, covering my hurt as best I could. Of course he's right. In the eyes of the Arabs I'm but a woman, fit to serve and never to command. And yet a queen once reigned here, holding all in her sway, all except the King at Jerusalem. I'm damned if I'll put up with this for long.

The men remained sequestered in the tent a goodly while. I made it a point of honour not to eavesdrop on their conversation and went for a walk with the boys. Hamid held my hand as we hunted lizards in the sand.

On my return I found the Sharif taking his leave, an obviously happy man. He rode at a gallop round our tent hotly pursued by his men, all whooping and firing their bullets across our bows. F. retired to rest with instructions that he should not be disturbed. And where the hell was Yūsuf who'd gone for water an hour ago and hadn't reappeared?

After he'd rested I came across him digging a hole near our tent with an ancient instrument he must have borrowed from the Bedu, a hole as big as a trench and he a sick man. From his fanatical appearance – he poured sweat, and several of the cuts had opened and bled afresh – I knew I must hold my tongue, and sauntered past without a word, merely observing from a distance that when he was satisfied he went for his mule and buried two of his boxes in the sand after pacing the distance between his hole and a peculiarly-formed tamarisk tree. He's up to his games again. I mustn't appear too curious or he'll fly into a sulk. Nothing changes, very much, in the end.

The house is empty, swept, and garnished. I could almost erect my tent and imagine that I slept outside . . . Hamid and Mahmūd took us to the edge of the village and then hung back. As gypsies of the desert they dared not enter . . . The house has anyway a touch of evil to it. Facing west, it rears above the walls to look across the flat-bottomed plain towards Sirwāh and the mountains. F. is much pleased and taken with a nervous restlessness. Yūsuf too is glad to have escaped the simple rigours of the desert. Only I am lost.

But there's much to be done. I've spoken with my so-called foreman, Sālih, to ascertain the men are present and more or less correct. We'll visit the ruins tomorrow so that I might explain my procedures and work shall start in earnest the day after that. The tools provided by the Sharif are adequate. I should be pleased. Instead I'm gravely discontent and wish we had stayed away from this miserable village where the women wheedle to share my daily bread and children follow silently *en masse*; and mangy dogs, covered in sores and a thick coating of dust.

F. sings from another room, an unexpected snatch of opera. I've not heard him sing since before Hajarah. Please God look over us, and watch.

I've crossed to the other side and shall remain for ever beyond reach of decent, ordinary folk. I can't say I'm sorry. All is written – I wouldn't change one word. My journey across the mountains had only this goal, for which I've waited so long, and patiently. He's made a woman of me at last.

F. sleeps now, his strong shoulders bare in the moonlight while I, unable to sleep, look around me with the eyes of one who has irrevocably changed. I listen to the piteous howling of the dogs, and wonder why I feel no shame.

F. rode with me to the ruins accompanied by the Sharif with whom he's become inexplicably as thick as thieves. They climbed directly on to the wall (not, I'm pleased to say, Michael's habitual spot), and watched us from a height as if we were their minions. I tried to concentrate on the business in hand.

First we must excavate the wall. The structure looks solid

enough and will consequently suffer little damage from in-experienced hands. The pillars are much more delicate. Until we've reached their foundations, I can't say how secure they are.

I've divided the men into three teams of eight (plus a dozen or so boys), some to dig and some to cart away the sand which we must deposit downwind else all our labours will come to naught. The roving sandstorms I'll deal with as best I can: one cannot plan for every eventuality. Sālih, as foreman, is excused all manual work. Today he spent more time huddled with the Sharif and F. than taking note of my orders. If I must get rid of him, he'll prove a mean adversary.

Yūsuf will organize the midday meal and have it brought on site. Now that he's returned to 'civilization', in a position of some authority over others, he's regained his better humours and no longer mopes about going home. I've also increased his wages and promised him another set of clothes.

Hamid visited us for a short time only. I asked him what had happened to Mahmūd who is apparently 'engaged'. The boy looked distinctly ill at ease. I caught him throwing stones quite deliberately at one of my men and had to chase him away. One plainly can't please all of the people all of the time.

And when the day's work was done – we've erected flimsy shelters thatched with brushwood and a matting of withered grasses – I let the men go and stayed for a time on my own, feeling more confident than I have for some time.

The men chant as they work, a plaintive dirge that recalls the song of the fishermen at Hodeidah. How far away that seems, and the good Dr Wendell. The mountains form a barrier twixt east and west, and in between a raging, beastly war, or maybe it's stopped, we can't tell out east. The Turk would never dare show his face here, on the other side of the mountains. We're safe, I think, from all external foe. Our enemies lie all within.

I slip from the blinding light of the desert into the darkness of my house, our house, for which I long most greedily throughout the interminable day. They say that all roads lead to Jerusalem. *But the unclean spirit, when he is gone out of the man, passeth through waterless places, seeking rest, and findeth it not* . . .

We were delayed several hours by a most unfortunate accident on site. Sālih had taken one of the groups to clear rubble from the eastern edge of the wall, small boulders, broken stones, the usual desultory fragments which mark man's presence in the universe, when one of the men let out the most curdled scream. He'd chopped himself through the foot with his hoe, the bloody piece hanging on by a thread. The men downed tools and gathered round, making a frightful hubbub. Much shaking of heads and rebellious looks in my direction, as if I were personally at fault. No one thought to blame Sālih who should have established that the men were at least competent before he put them to work.

My petticoats were once again called into service. I never thought a man could bleed so much from his extremities. The sand ran darkly red. I lent my mule to carry him back to the village and would have followed on foot had not Sālih said I risked a stoning if I tried. After this, the men stayed long at their prayers, first washing their bodies in the dry dust before prostrating themselves in rag-tag rows behind my pillars.

Deciding it would be unwise to hurry them, I concentrated instead on sketching a map of the site as it exists today. One soon forgets the boundaries of the known. The rest of the day passed without incident and my men trudged wearily home at sundown, discouraged by unaccustomed work.

As we neared the village I felt my spirits soar. F. had prepared a feast which we ate in the upper room, seated on the floor. He bade me wear my nightdress, open at the front like all the whores of Mesopotamia, and called in Yūsuf on the pretext that he wanted wine. Yūsuf entered reluctantly, keeping his eyes on the floor. I spoke to him. He wouldn't answer nor would he look at me. I rose slowly to take the bottle from his hands. My nightdress billowed as I moved. He must have seen my breasts. I wanted him to see; I wanted him to know that I am mistress here and that I give myself gladly to the man I love.

So it has come to this. And still I beg for more.

My temple has become a hive of extraordinary activity, Egyptian in scope, that rivals the construction of the pyramids. To his credit, the Sharif has provided six pairs of oxen and conjured up more men and boys from his followers, all on the face of it in reasonable health. These new recruits I've put to work on the peristyle hall where their progress is remarkable.

As Sālih's empire grows, he becomes more unscrupulous than ever. I've heard rumours that he helps himself to a portion of each man's pay. I dare not rock my boat but still must find a way of cutting him down to size.

The Sharif and F. paid us a visit soon after the noonday prayers when the men had just returned to work. Tools were downed in a trice and my entire workforce stood to attention in the shadowless sun while the Sharif inspected a pile of inscribed tablets with all the perspicacity of a mole. I ordered Sālih to get the men moving again. When he refused I walked across the inner court to speak with F. who must not come here unannounced. He said he would come and go as he pleased, being answerable to no one.

I was relieved when the pair decided they'd seen enough and Sālih took them off site. He remained at least one hour away. On his return he moved some of my men from the north-east corner of the hall and put them to work at the west. Claiming that these were orders from Mr Fergusson, he refused point-blank to revert to my original instructions. I was forced, reluctantly, to shift around the other teams as the north-east corner provides the most logical point of entry into the hall and I believe one should always progress in a logical way.

My faithful Hamid has recovered some of his cheerfulness and even Mahmūd showed his face fleetingly. They follow me like dogs and have stopped throwing stones.

F. talked to me last night, after we were done. I hadn't realized how little we say to each other. He's like an Arab himself, to whom body and spirit are forever opposed. He talked to me about Shehārah and his dreams. He told me – but this is terrible – that after he'd caught wind of a murderous plot among the Imam's men, he escaped with 'Ali down the mountain and killed him in cold blood as soon as they reached the plains, suspecting, he said, that 'Ali had conspired to rob and murder him with the rest.

What should I mourn more, 'Ali's death or our own complicity? I asked him how he could kill a man, a follower and friend, for the merest hint of suspicion at something that may or may not be.

'It's not enough to survive,' he said with a new kind of weariness. 'I have to win in the end.'

And after he slept, I listened to the wind blowing in from the desert across those waterless places, and knew that what is written is invariably true. *Even so shall it be also unto this evil generation.*

As it is Friday, another lost day, I rose late, no more refreshed than usual, and took Yūsuf with me to the ruins, requiring his help to undertake some measurements which cannot be done amidst the bustle of a working day. Michael met us some way off: he looked agitated, and waved his arms around as if to hurry us along.

When we reached the outer wall, I understood his concern. A number of workmen dug frantically on their own account in a spot to the east of the temple wall. If they put such efforts into their paid employment we'd be finished in two winks of an eye. As Yūsuf had positioned himself firmly behind me, the job of scaring them away was left to me. I fired my pistol into the sky and spurred my mule into a very uneven chase.

The damage in fact was slight. They appear to have discovered the entrance to some tombs, a mausoleum, perhaps, which I must closely guard to keep at bay the scavenging hordes. But to whom can I entrust the task? Yūsuf rolled his eyes a lot and claimed the place simply crawled with 'afrits. He could not, would not be the one. It's hard to say whether he truly believes such stuff and nonsense but his performance was sufficiently theatrical to convince me that an unwilling dog is worse than no dog at all.

I turned to Michael as my only hope and told him what was required without, I must say, making the faintest impression. For all I know he may be deaf and stupid as well as mute because he continued to squat on his haunches exactly where he has always done. I'll order the speedy completion of the grave diggers' work so that my expedition may reap its proper rewards.

On reaching the ruins this morning straight after breakfast I was astonished to find that work had already commenced. Indeed, it must have commenced before dawn because the whole site moved with a rhythmical precision that comes when each man and boy carries out his allotted task in the prescribed manner, the oxen too, instead of milling about like casual guests at a funeral party which has been the dominant impression so far. The sight filled me with dread, a sure sign that I am losing control.

Michael has moved a little closer to the probable site of Sheba's mausoleum. Perhaps he understood me after all.

F. talked last night about his sister Isobel, who lives in Glasgow where she makes ends meet by running a haberdashery off Sauchiehall Street. From the evidence of her photograph she's about twenty-five, and while not pretty has a brooding sultriness that some men prefer. A shame her eyes protrude so.

'She must be very worried about you,' I said.

'She doesn't care one way or the other. In all the time I've been in these parts, I've ached to hear news of her. A dozen letters was all she could afford. A dozen miserable letters in four long years. It's not much, is it? But I care, Elinor, I care enough for all of them.'

'I'm sure you're much too hard on her. She must be very busy. A haberdashery, you know . . . '

'I've had enough, Elinor. I'm quitting as soon as we're done. If I stay any longer, I'll be as doltish as the rest of them.'

'But what will you do? I mean, now that you've lost your savings, you can't return to the business of clerking. My father perhaps could find you something. Something more agreeable.'

Contempt showed plainly in his eyes. 'Your father,' he said, 'can distribute his gracious crumbs elsewhere.'

He looked at me then as if he hated me. It's not my fault the cards have been unfairly dealt. He doesn't realize that to give is as good as to receive. If only he'd let me come closer, I could tell him this and make him understand. He needles me for sport and hurts me as surely as the blows he struck at 'Ali.

And yet my heart goes out to him. He wants more than anything in the world to return to a place he calls home, a place in which, by his own admission, no one cares for him, while I, who love my home and all its occupants, have forfeited my right to belong. These cruel lands are my lands now and Maunton but an insubstantial dream. Like Yūsuf I tremble at the spirits of this place, and all their deadly intrigues.

Today we reached the entrance to the tombs, eleven in all, one much smaller than the rest which must have housed the body of a child. Their treasures amount to precisely this: a few human bones of indeterminate age, the entire skeleton of a goat, shards of rather inferior pottery, a fragment of bull's head frieze from what I take to be a funerary stele, a bronze ass with dedicatory inscription, and a handful of silver coins that must have slipped from grasping fingers in the dark. The boundaries of scholarship are scarcely advanced. I should have left the would-be looters to continue the work at their own convenience.

In spite of my trials, the temple rises slowly from the sands in all its former magnificence.

The peristyle hall is a wonder to behold. It measures approximately sixty feet by seventy-two: we've dug to a depth of thirty feet. The line of eight pillars evident when I first visited the site stands apart from the main structure which has two openings, one into the temple proper, while the second (in the north-east corner, as I had anticipated) leads up some steps into an outer court. The hall itself is lined with thirty-two pillars, behind which, on two sides, stands a most curious wall containing a series of false windows of imitation lattice, cut in stone and miraculously preserved under the weight of sand.

An inscription found near the entrance confirms the temple's dedication to the Moon God, Ilumquh, thus explaining the presence of so many bulls' heads and spouting drains to catch the blood of slaughtered beasts. It also explains why I felt so peculiar that night I stood here under the moon, that sudden rush of exultation. One does not need to dig to feel the sanctity of stones.

I've made several drawings and am currently preoccupied with determining the hall's probable roof structure. I wish only that my companion shared my interest in these problems. He looks vexed whenever I seek his opinion and says they're all stones to him. Our life together frightens me. We meet as strangers, even at our most intimate moments, with all the shock that strangeness brings.

The Sharif has returned to his old ways, demanding more money for the men and facilities he has put at my disposal. A rogue if ever I saw one but one who holds the cards and knows full well that I must keep him sweet.

The bargaining took place on site with Sālih sniffing about our heels, ever eager when material matters come to the fore. I told him quite honestly that my coffers are virtually bare. I've enough to honour my original agreement with him but little surplus fat, and can scarcely wire for more in present circumstances. I must thank Yūsuf for the Sharif's obvious incredulity. He's apparently depicted me as a lump of pure ambergris from which the Sharif proposes to take what he can.

When he understood at last that no meant no, he staked his claim to every single stone and artefact, each broken head and tablet of inscription, each priceless trinket unearthed by our labours. I laughed at his preposterous request and said I couldn't negotiate on an empty stomach.

'Anyway,' I asked, 'what will you do with all my bits and bobs?' He didn't know, of course. Although he plainly sees how much I value them, he doesn't know why and doubtless assumes they have an everyday currency, else why would he covet them?

'They belong to my people,' he said, at which Sālih nodded in vigorous agreement. 'You have no rights to them.'

'My dear Sharif,' I replied as patiently as I could, 'they belong to history. Scholars from all corners of the globe must be given a chance to examine their significance. We're not in the dark ages now.'

'They're *mine*,' he repeated, like a spoilt child.

Breaking off our discussion, he rode his mare around the base of the wall to a pile of stones and Sabaean inscriptions which I haven't deciphered yet and ordered a posse of men to cart the whole lot back to Māreb. One of the stones, carved with ibex heads, was truly enormous.

Two can play at his little games. I'll make sure that he's offered only the heaviest takings so that he may quickly regret the effort involved in satisfying his greed.

Another day of rest and forced inactivity. I've come to dread them utterly. Bereft of work, I am no one. To give myself something to do, I took my *Qur'ān* to the ruins, wishing to read again the story of Sheba's visit to Solomon. I read it aloud to Michael, my deaf-mute audience. As I came to its perplexing end when Sheba, mistaking the glass paving of the courtyard for a stream, lifts up her skirts and thus exposes her legs before the King, I had the most terrible vision of my dear sister Jane, the sweetest thing imaginable, unsullied, lifting up her skirts to Fergusson the King.

These waking dreams are far more terrible than those of the night, which one shakes off like water from a dog, and blames on over-tiredness, or a diet too rich, but not these dreamings of the day which breed within the darkest corners of one's own imagination. He can take my body as he chooses to satisfy his lust, or his love. That's part of the bargain between us. Unspoken, true, but a bargain nonetheless to which we are willing partners and from which I gain as much as he does because it's *my* choice too. But Jane . . . I must not do this to her.

At last we have some news of the war. One of the Sharif's many relatives returned home last night to the sound of much noisy rejoicing and firing of guns into the sky. By morning, word had spread through the village that the Imam's revolt is close to collapse. Having relieved the siege of Menākhah, a Turkish force now fights its way to the walls of San'ā where the Vali sits like a goose, making occasional forays against the rebels and returning with a booty of assorted heads which he skewers on pikes around the walls to set the townsfolk a good example.

The news has turned the Sharif into a bigger bully than ever. This morning he entered our house when I was scarcely dressed, accompanied by three harmless ruffians whom he introduced as my guard.

'I don't need a guard,' I said. 'I'm perfectly safe.'

'For your protection,' said the Sharif stubbornly.

'Protection from what? No one threatens me.'

'You'll do as you're bid,' said F., who'd come into the room half-clothed.

I argued with him. The notion of a guard is ridiculous. My relations with the men are good; even Sālih and I are on relative speaking terms. The guards are sent to spy on me, nothing less, and it's monstrously unjust to expect me to pay for that.

One cannot parry force with reason. It's as if F. and the Sharif are in league to bleed me of everything I have. I've sprung three shadows in addition to my own and must endure their inconvenience as I do everything else.

If the Sharif has openly declared himself my enemy, I wonder what's become of my friends. Yūsuf has fallen sick from a sort of sand-fly fever. He's covered in sores and moans more persistently than usual. Hamid and Mahmūd have turned their faces away. I miss them, honestly.

As for F., two beasts are lodged within his breast, the beast of the night and the beast of the day, which vie with each other to make my life more of a misery. I've chosen this bed, and so must lie on it gladly, which I do, of course, damned if I'll be made his victim. But I wish that, when I return to him at night, wearied from my labours and the sweat of bending a recalcitrant workforce to my will, we could bridge the silence that spreads its icy waters between us, break down the walls of secrecy that hide our inner thoughts and actions. Or maybe we have no thoughts. Maybe we are indeed these mechanical gestures that pass for human intercourse. I have become an empty room that only he can fill.

His beast of the day wears a different face. It's like a gargoyle whose features have been washed away. Does he grimace or leer? Is he evil or kind or – worst of all – indifferent? We stand on different sides and I prefer the Sharif for my enemy, whose game at least one understands.

Despite my entreaties, F. came again to the ruins and after a brief tour of inspection ordered Sālih – in front of me – to start work at once on the line of free-standing pillars beyond the hall. I told him this was nonsense. We should work slowly outwards from the main structure and must design supports before we so much as touch the pillars. Such tasks require a very special consideration and should be left till last.

'They've stood these thousand years.'

'Two thousand,' I corrected, 'at least.'

'They look pretty solid to me. It's about time someone made some damned progress around here.'

'You don't understand. It's all very delicate.'

'I'll be the judge, Miss Grace, of what I do or do not understand.'

Oh yes, he called me Miss Grace, like a slap in the face. And while we argued, heatedly, Sālih obeyed his commands with an alacrity he's never shown towards me. After one of the better teams had assembled at the pillars he looked to me to give the men their instructions.

'Ask Mr Fergusson,' I said. 'He seems to know this business better than I.'

I turned my back on them and went off for a walk, trailed by my guards who wilted in the sun. The last I saw was Mr Fergusson standing on a broken stone, like a soap box, giving out orders that rightly belong to me.

With all this quarrelling, I'm sick at heart. F. leaves me alone; I hear him pacing in the dark, from room to empty room, taken with a restlessness that has infected us all. Sleep passes over this house as surely as if it were marked with a sign, a bloody cross, the sign of chosen ones, but chosen for what? Our fate was concocted in hell and we are merely acting out our parts as Lucifer would wish. I cannot take much more.

The endless activity of my days is directed towards the wrong end. Right from the start I knew we shouldn't meddle with this place. That though the stones have silted up with sands, the gardens of Saba laid waste, their gods have not deserted them. And gods are stronger than men. They shall, I know, rise up to answer our provocation.

For these are Sheba's lands. Of course the dates are wrong. Of course it's historically impossible. Of course, if a Queen of Sheba ever paid a visit to Solomon, she never came from here. This city was built long after Solomon's lifetime. She came from the north. Only later writers became confused and called her the Queen of the South, who shall rise up in the judgement with this generation to condemn it, utterly. I know all this, and yet I know also that myth is stronger than the truth. He said that to me once. He's right. He's always right.

But the unclean spirit, when he is gone out of the man, passeth through waterless places, seeking rest, and findeth it not. Then he saith, I will return into my house whence I came out; and when he is come, he findeth it empty, swept, and garnished. Then goeth he,

*and taketh with himself seven other spirits more evil than himself,
and they enter in and dwell there: and the last state of that man
becometh worse than the first. Even so shall it be also unto this evil
generation.*

I wonder why they stopped at seven. Our dwelling place
could house a thousand spirits and still have room for more.
We should erect a sign above the door: 'Spirits wanted, the
wickeder the better'. God knows, there's plenty of opportunity here.

How strange. The house is suddenly thrown into silence.
What's happened to Yūsuf? He's stopped moaning. The
guards are quiet too, and F. No footsteps. Where is he? Have
they abandoned me? I'll not be frightened if they have. The
house feels peaceful, as if the storm has passed. Upon my floor
a patch of moonlight grows. The light is ghostly pale.

Did Sheba worship the moon? Did she graze her flocks
beneath its beneficent light? Did she believe, as they still do,
that Ilumquh distils the dew and causes vegetation to grow,
and that the sun it is that wishes to destroy us all? Then why
did she swap her gods for Solomon's? Is that why the temple
fell?

Such peacefulness invites me to sleep. I shall stretch out my
aching body in the patch of moonlight and wait for the healing
to start.

Sleep works wonders on the tired mind. I felt quite eager when
I awoke this morning, as if I knew already what the day might
hold in store. I even managed to exchange a few civil words
with my guards, who find their duty as irksome as I do.
They'd be far happier shooting a few Turks, or rebels – I still
can't fathom which side these people are on.

The three are not from Māreb but rather from an Ashrāf

clan centred around Harib, two days' journey away. Apparently, the Sharif is related to their leader, though not, it seems, on very good terms with him. They look almost Indian with fairer skin and straighter hair than the tribes around here.

Anyway, they're not such bad sorts when one makes their acquaintance, apart from their dreadful smell which emanates from the rancid oil smeared across their bodies. At least one always knows where they are, even when they lurk behind corners. Their names are Hasan, Fārid and Ibrāhīm, but to myself I call them the three musketeers.

They're not, I'm glad to say, particularly bright, and have assumed that as a woman I'm an easy bird to stalk. This is just as well because when we reached the ruins, somewhat ahead of the main party, Michael flailed his arms in an obvious attempt to attract my attention. I managed to head them off in the other direction by suggesting that I'd caught sight of an intruder in the scrub and went to see for myself what was wrong.

Michael lost no time in making known his discovery. She lay tucked in a corner of the mausoleum, buried most unusually into the wall behind a limestone stele depicting bulls' heads and rams. I recognized at once her significance and would have embraced the man had he stopped jigging for a moment. Communicating in sign language, I told him he must guard her with his life until I could find some means of sneaking her away from our common foe.

The day dragged on and on. Michael took my instructions literally and barred the way most ostentatiously to anyone who attempted to cross into the tombs. This wouldn't do at all. I had to bully some discretion into him, and eventually ordered him back to the wall where he might blend again with his surroundings.

Sālih badgered me with questions about Mr Fergusson's pillars. I told him I'd washed my hands of the whole affair. If Mr Fergusson, against my advice, has chosen to start the work

at this particular juncture, he must see to the consequences
himself. Yes, the pillars undoubtedly need support and no, I
hadn't worked out what form this should take.

Adding to my burdens, a fight broke out in the late morning, started, I think, by Fārid who picked a quarrel with the
sickliest specimen of my entire force, one who earns his keep
by flopping in whatever shade he can find and scraping
half-heartedly in the dirt. I'd have dismissed him long ago
were he not related – as they all are – to my blessed Sharif.

Our comedy of the morning was probably a re-enactment
of a centuries-old feud whose origins are obscure. They went
at one another hammer and tongs, my three unlikely guards
and a faction of the workforce who'd sprung to the sickly one's
defence.

In the event, this truculence was heaven-sent as it allowed
me (with Sālih's consent) to pack my guards off home in
disgrace, leaving the field free to rescue Michael's find. It was
nonetheless imperative to maintain a front of the utmost
secrecy because of the Sharif's latter-day interest in all things
archaeological.

My plan was this. I took one of Yūsuf's luncheon baskets,
its contents covered with a napkin, and personally distributed
a portion of the victuals to the men. Overcome with faintness
on my return, I stepped into the shade of the mausoleum,
calling to Sālih that I was quite all right. He wasn't to worry on
my account.

The deed was quickly done. I found the spot where we had
hidden her, placed her face-down in my basket (she fitted
exactly, the only problem being that she weighed considerably
more than a score of flat, Arab loaves), covered her with the
napkin and, after a suitable interval, emerged refreshed from
the tombs. I felt Sālih's crafty eyes upon me and knew that I
must give no hint of the terrible load in my basket. To carry a
solid lump of alabaster as if it were air is no mean feat; the strain
clearly showed. Sālih came over expressly to enquire after my

health, a concern I would have welcomed were it not so beastly inconvenient. I sent him away with thanks.

Then I realized that my action was premature. The whole afternoon and early evening stretched ahead of me and here I was, metaphorically chained to a basket whose contents no one else must see. Sketching was my answer to this, as it is to many of life's tribulations. Not only does it impart an aura of activity but the act of drawing lines on a blank page is immensely refreshing to the spirits. Draughtsmanship is, after scholarship, my preferred occupation. And so I spent a happy afternoon recording progress on the distant pillars which represent a fine example of pre-Islamic genius.

An hour before sundown I left the site, telling Sālih I felt a trifle weak. He watched me swing my basket on to the withers of my mule, which let out a bray of protest at the unaccustomed weight, and asked if I wouldn't prefer to leave the basket behind with the rest of the day's utensils.

'No thank you, Sālih,' I said hurriedly. 'My sketching things . . . It's quite all right. I need a container.'

The man's no fool. I wonder what he knows.

I entered Māreb as the sun dipped behind the mountains. The women went about their business in the dusty streets. I thought I caught sight of Hamid slipping between the houses. It must have been one of the other boys; he never comes here. My three disgraced guards chewed *kat* in the doorway. I went directly to my room where I took the head from my basket and laid it reverentially on the floor.

She stared up at me, the alabaster head of a woman, a perfect oval, its top truncated by her hairline. Slim, elongated nose; a mouth no wider than the nostrils; each eye a perfect ellipse lined starkly in black, as were the pupils and the thick eyebrows cut in a straight line across her forehead.

For you, my Queen, I've travelled from the Red Sea to Shehārah and down again into the barren wastes of a land whose blighted hopes bear witness to God's punishment of man. Your one true likeness I hold between my hands. You came from the ends of the earth to hear the wisdom of Solomon, bearing great gifts, an hundred and twenty talents of gold, and of spices very great store and precious stones. All these you gave to Solomon. And then you turned and went back into your own land, where I have come at last, to claim you as my prize, certain in the knowledge that, whatever happens to me now, whatever fates the Gods have engineered for me, my journey shall be deemed a success.

Disturbed by sudden sounds within the house, I looked around for a hiding place. Finding a weakness in the mud and wattle floor, I hastily stuffed the Queen in her napkin and hid her in the cavity. Not a moment too soon. F. burst into the room, looking frightfully unkempt as if he'd spent the day in a tavern. His face fell when he saw me.

'It's you, I thought . . . Never mind.' He stared at my clothes, more than usually soiled from the filthy floor. 'Can't you keep yourself clean?' he said sharply. 'And the house. I've known better in the dens of Aden. Or do you enjoy living like a Jew? Why the hell doesn't Yūsuf earn his keep for a change? A dog would be more use to us.'

'Yūsuf's sick. From sand-fly fever.'

He stepped closer.

'What are you doing?'

'A nest of ants, I thought. We've been troubled for some time.'

'Let me see.'

'It's nothing.'

'Clean yourself up before we eat. You'll put me off my food.'

After he'd gone I burst into tears, upset by the narrowness of my escape as much as by his cruel words. I tremble to think what would have happened if he'd found the head. He'd probably sell it to the Sharif for a few sovereigns more.

A most curious thing happened today on the way to the ruins; I wish I knew what it meant. It's rung the tocsin for sure.

As we left the village I noticed we were shadowed by an adolescent boy, lean-looking even for a Yemeni, who staggered from exhaustion. I took him for an idiot. My men threw stones to frighten him away.

Half a mile further on he reappeared ahead of us and made a last, shaky spurt towards me. I threw him some coins, hoping to mollify him with alms. As I shouted for help, he thrust a note into my skirts. It nearly missed. With that he salaamed in the sand and cantered off.

I hid the note in my pocket and must wait until I had a moment to myself before I could acquaint myself with its contents. On site, there were the usual problems to resolve and disagreements to quell so that by the time I found myself alone I was eaten alive with curiosity. The note, badly typed, had been sealed with wax and bore the imprint of a thumb rather than any more official seal. It was also unsigned:

Dear Miss Grace, I beg you most urgently to return to base at your earliest opportunity. Your flight into the interior may yet unleash an international storm. You-know-who are showing interest again, now that they're getting back on top. I can't hang on much longer, especially as our own side aren't exactly amused, either. They're convinced I'm mixed up in this business and have started to throw the book at me. More bad news, I'm afraid. Kincaid at Aden has made enquiries about a mutual acquaintance who is not, apparently, all he's cracked up to be. If he tries to get in touch, run for your life. Trust no one, my dear, and God speed.

I recognized the hand of Dr Wendell. In spite of his intended anonymity, he gave himself away with every word. And, though the note was designed to shock me to my senses (God knows, I lost those months ago), I wondered instead at the man's incalculable worth. If the note had fallen into the wrong hands, he faced instant dismissal. I am, it seems, *persona non grata* with everyone.

For my sins, I showed the note to F. as soon as I returned home, a gesture of unpremeditated spite because I wanted to hit out at him, to show him that he'd lost my esteem and that of others, including our dear friend at Hodeidah.

Water off the usual duck's back. 'Will you run,' he sneered, 'as the doctor suggests?'

'There's work to be done,' I replied. 'I'll stay as long as I must.'

'A martyr to history.'

'You can't hurt me now. He must have meant you. You're our only mutual acquaintance. But he knows we travelled together. That's odd. If we travel together, we're already in touch. And why should Aden make enquiries about you? What have you done?'

'I could think of a thousand things, and it's probably something else.'

He went out after supper and stayed away all night. I sat some time with Yūsuf, who grows a little stronger from my ministrations. And soon to bed, knowing that in one corner of my room I have the wealth of all Arabia.

My temple echoes to the footsteps of the Gods. Are we tainted by their senseless cruelty?

My guards, the three musketeers, took it into their heads to lay upon Michael, beating him about the head and limbs with the butts of their musket guns. I did what I could to intervene but by the time they'd finished he lay like a bloody foetus at my feet. They've smashed his teeth, several bones of his body, and turned his legs to pulp. Most horribly of all, he let them do it to him; as they rained their blows upon him, he gave no cry for help, no sound beyond a strangled gurgling, and in his eyes that look of resignation, the unshakeable belief that all is Allah's will.

They stopped as suddenly as they'd begun and walked away, talking among themselves as calmly if they'd just squashed a lizard. Fārid spat when I confronted him. Michael, he claims, is an outcast, stripped of any rights. They can do with him what they choose. My protests they blatantly ignored, and Sālih warned I must not interfere. They live by their own rules here.

I turned my attentions to Michael who dragged his battered body down into the temple, drawn by some atavistic memory that, once he'd entered its sanctuary, Bilqīs, my Queen of Sheba, would look over him and watch. They couldn't harm him there. Or rather, I tried to attend to him. He looked at me so fearfully wild, a wounded beast that creeps into its lair, and wouldn't let me approach.

This episode has left me sorely shaken. It seems I have outlived my usefulness and can neither protect my friends nor patch them when they bleed. They say that Iblis is the greatest of the *jinn*. His name in English means Despair.

I write this at my window looking out at the dust storms which swirl across the plains. The hazy light has swallowed up the mountains. My house is peaceful after yesterday's up-heavals. Yūsuf has gone to the ruins in my stead, bearing a message for Sālih that I find myself indisposed. I had to shout to raise him from his sickbed. He's neither more nor less sick than the rest of us and cannot be excused.

The odd thing is that I feel so calm, so composed, as I tread daintily through the tumbled ruins of my life. It matters little that the Gods have forsaken me.

It's funny, really, how after each dreadful day has come and gone one thinks – attempting to look on the bright side – that the morrow can only improve. It doesn't, does it? Things never improve if one retains capacity for hope.

I would like to think, nonetheless, that whatever the future holds I'll never experience another day like yesterday.

There I go again, drowning out my chances with the cracked bells of hope.

And yet I find that I can write about what happened with a spirit of detachment, as if it happened to another and I'm merely recording the facts. Perhaps I, too, am falling victim to the resignation so beloved of a True Believer. Let me set the record straight regarding yesterday which, if it's not to be the worst day of my life, comes pretty near the bottom of anyone's book.

My start to the ruins was delayed by an altercation with the Sharif who had heard (from Sālih?) that I may have salted away some of the ruins' most precious finds. With a clean heart I told him this was nonsense. There are no hiding places on site and even if he searched my house from top to bottom he'd find I spoke the truth. I had, of course, firmly sealed my precious queen within the floor.

We argued for an hour or more until finally I said he was barking up the wrong tree. If he thought he was being cheated he should ask Sālih how much he pocketed each week from the men's wages. Although this money is, strictly speaking, mine, I would prefer to see it more fairly distributed among the Sharif's impoverished followers instead of disappearing into the bottomless pocket of their foreman, whose growing fortune may be put to bad use. Telling tales is not usually my game but frankly I'd had more than enough of all of them.

Believing that I'd regained the upper hand, I rode out to the ruins in a more cheerful frame of mind than usual. My good humour was quickly dissipated when I discovered that Sālih had ordered even more men to start work on the pillars. At least five feet of sand had been removed from their base and, while he's fashioned a supporting structure of sorts, the whole row sways in the breeze. One sneeze and it'll all fall down.

Although I've washed my hands of this piece of lunacy, I don't care to see my efforts destroyed by another's stubborn disregard of all things sensible.

My conversation with Sālih was brief and to the point. I asked him on whose authority he had increased the team at work on the pillars. Mr Fergusson's, of course. I told him that as I headed the excavations he must order the men to stop work immediately so that I might develop some proper supports. Men's lives were at stake, over and above my reputation. Sālih refused. I'd expected nothing better of him.

Knowing that I must finally confront F., I turned my mule back towards Māreb, a journey the confused beast completed in record time, assuming that the day's work was done. My guards had trouble keeping up with me.

Back in the village I marched up to the house where I went straight to his room. The door was bolted from the inside. Did I know then what he was up to, within? Beside myself with rage, I shouted through the door that he must show himself at once. I'd wait as long as I must, but wait I would.

My guards had followed me upstairs, drawn by the drama that unfolded before their puzzled eyes. They were not disappointed in its salacity. After some considerable time, during which we heard muffled scufflings, the door was unlocked and two brown bodies shot straight past me, quicker than the wind, brushing my skirts and taking the stairs in flight, hoping thus to conceal their identities; and though I saw only a flash of skin, those two shaved heads, I'd know the pair anywhere.

Faithless gypsies of the desert, how could you do this to me? You, of all people?

When the dust had settled, F. himself appeared at the door. He wore his trousers unbuckled, and a shirt open to the waist. My guards stepped back towards the stairs, alerted by that look in his eyes, a subterranean eddy of all the darker emotions known to man, ready to spew forth and sweep us over the brink.

The narrow doorway forced him to stoop. Even so, he towered above me. Eyes red as coals. Like a monstrous shadowplay he grew in size, this dark, satanic shape, lost all sense of human form. Shoot your shadow if you must but never assume that it belongs to you. He said that to me once. Now, before my eyes, his shadow finally shook free. It swirled about my skirts, burning like a desert wind.

I caught my breath. That unmistakable tang of saltpetre. I felt myself choking, choking on the flames. Words lose all meaning when you reach the bottom, as we had. Certain actions can never be parcelled up in explanations, however hard one tries. His hand upon my shoulder. The shock of contact; my flesh seared where he touched me. An underside of grey to his beard. His mouth on mine, a forked tongue thrusting down my throat.

He pulled me roughly inside. We slammed the door. The sound of feet tumbling down the stairs, my guards who ran to save their souls, out towards the light, while we were trapped for all eternity.

The squalid room was strewn with clothes and blankets, evidence of his debaucheries. I let him come to me. My hair he first unleashed. It fell about my shoulders. I felt a queen again. Then he tore away my clothes until I stood for him in all my nakedness. That's how it's been and always shall be. I'd lost all sense of shame. Whatever he did to me I'd show him it was not enough. I'd walk unscorched through the fire of his initiation; I'd always survive and as a woman I would not break.

The things he did to me, there on the filthy floor. I never knew the depths to which a man could sink. I cried out in pain as he hurt me, cried exultantly as he forced on me each new indignity, the ways of Sodom and its beastly inhabitant. My legs spread on the floor. This beast upon my back. They must have heard me at the gates of hell. He's never done this to a woman. Never. I am a maiden again. His slave. He's bought my body for his pleasure. Then why does he weep? Why do I want this pain? Why do I long to submit again and rejoice in my debasement? Why, when I would have loved him gently, do I long for the demon in him to rise up again, snarling as he rips into my softer flesh, my underbelly?

He broke before I did. He broke before I had finished and threw himself into a corner, his face hid in a blanket. I wanted him still. I crawled towards him and begged him to take me again. Any way he chose. I was his, couldn't he see that? We'd walked through the fires together. He tried to shake me off but I clung to him like a shipwrecked sailor who dares not let go of his raft; who sees a solitary seagull and thinks, poor idiot, that help is close at hand.

Outside the harsh white light. The sound of children shrieking at their games. The yelping of a dog. His back was turned to me. I covered it with my hair and felt a weariness lapping at my body, hurt and broken from the things he'd done to me. The raft was slipping my grasp. I tried to hold on; the water was black and icy cold. It numbed my limbs. I couldn't keep afloat much longer. The currents pulled me down. Let go. You've reached the end. No strength to fight any more. It's done.

And, just as I let go, I felt his hand reaching across the floor, the fingers interlaced with mine, gently at first then with a grip that all but crushed my bones. Like two lost souls we clung to each other, victims of the storm, and pushed ourselves off into the sea's dark swell. The waters closed above our heads as together we sank into the deep.

It's over here, for me. He looks at me askance, expecting a woman's recriminations, and quits the room as soon as I appear, seeing in me a witness to his depravity. Even in this he will not treat me as an equal partner.

What's done is done. I'll take Dr Wendell's advice and cross once more those perilous mountains that stand between me and the civilized world. The journey will be hard as I must travel alone. One task alone detains me. Before I leave I'll make a full and detailed drawing of Sheba's temple, which so far I've attempted piece by piece. My final act shall be to fit the pieces together so that the world may know the full splendour of her earthly kingdom and the joys of heaven to come.

Too late. Why do our good intentions always arise too late? My task is finished, before it was ever begun.

★

12 April 1911   *British Vice-Consulate,*
                                   Hodeidah & Cameran

The Right Honourable Sir G. A. Lowther, KCMG, CB,
His Majesty's Ambassador, Constantinople

Sir,

I have the honour to confirm my cablegram of the 8th instant, informing Your Excellency of the relief of SAN'Ā on the 4th by a force under COL. RIZA BEY.

It would appear that the above force encountered no resistance whatever in entering SAN'Ā itself, the Arabs who were apparently in some strength in the heights to the south having hastily retreated northwards.

General 'IZZET PASHA with the main army comprising some fifteen infantry battalions and several guns arrived at SAN'Ā on the following afternoon.

The relief of the capital was celebrated with general rejoicings, and a grand review of all the troops in the garrison was held by 'IZZET PASHA on the morning of the 6th.

As regards losses sustained by the garrison during the siege, I learn from a fairly reliable source that the total number of wounded admitted into hospital since the siege amounted to forty-three. The number of men killed during the various sorties made did not exceed fifty or sixty, and the total casualties 200.

My informant criticizes the arrangements made by the Turks for the defence of the town of SAN'Ā where, with a force of considerably below 6,000 all told, they tried to defend a perimeter of twelve kilometres. In his opinion, it was indeed possible for the Arabs to have taken the place by assault at any time if they were able to use their guns.

The rifle shooting of the troops was very poor and their artillery practice worse. I am able to confirm the above opinion from my experience up at SAN'Ā. The Turks burst their time shrapnel about a thousand feet in the air, where it was quite harmless to perhaps anything but an aeroplane. The common shell used has very little effect on the houses and towers round about SAN'Ā. It would appear that in a single day, MOHAMMED 'ALI's force fired off at least 3,000 shells in the bombardment of SHAOOB, and on other occasions but little less, disposing of barely two or three hundred Arabs.

The enemy, on the other hand, had not the vaguest idea of making war, nor had they any particular plan of campaign.

Without the slightest pretence to cohesion, the Arabs do not pay the least attention to the orders of the Imam or to those of their leaders. Each man fights independently as he thinks fit, his chief object being to avoid risking his 'skin' any more than he can possibly help. What appeared to have scared the Arab rebels most were dynamite cartridges with a friction fuse attached, which the Turks laid down at intervals all round the walls of the town. A shepherd one day trod on one of these which immediately exploded and blew him up, making the enemy very cautious about approaching the walls thereafter.

Throughout the siege, there appears to have been no particular scarcity of supplies, the authorities having taken the timely precaution of laying in a plentiful stock of grains and other foodstuffs during the past year when the crops were abundant.

With truth and great respect,
I have the honour to be,
Sir,
Your Excellency's most obedient humble servant,
His Majesty's Vice-Consul at Hodeidah

★

F. sits in the window recess, his head encircled by shafts of pure white light. He's draped himself in one of Yūsuf's kilts which barely covers his thighs. He hums to himself a snatch of Verdi, tapping the rhythm on the floor; and when he sees me watching him he beckons, amused. I'll go to him presently as soon as I scent the man in him again.

Yūsuf suffers badly, I'm afraid. Like ourselves he's barricaded into his room, much given to whimpering. At night we hear him sniffling and howling at the moon like some poor lunatic. Having failed to comfort him, I am resigned to his infernal din.

I remember the silence after it had happened, a most surprised silence, the silence of the world's end which shall, God knows, take each one of us by surprise, however persistently its imminence is foretold. And in that silence I felt a certain wonder at the awful spectacle, before the shouting began.

We're locked in the house together, day after lifelong day. The Sharif means it as a punishment but it's the sweetest gift that any puffed-up lordling could bestow. I take the blame for everything and do so willingly. If our catastrophe has brought him back to me, into my arms and bed, I'll take a thousand punishments and turn my cheek for more. Defeat has stared us in the face. Our cupboards are stripped bare of everything down to the last vestige of my professional reputation. Our lives alone remain and they're of very minor coin. The effect on F. is remarkable. He could not be more kind and lets me come to him, flashing with his old sparkle as he squats like a native among the stinking rags of our captivity. He has become again the man who swaggered through the *sūqs* of Aden, fearless and bold, ready to lay his bets anew.

We talk of what we shall do if we ever make it to the other

side. I humour him but really cannot see that we shall ever escape the walls of our prison house. Nor do I look for release. I'm happy, at last. He says I have become another, more radiant by far; for him I glow with pride, undeterred by my lack of an ordinary prettiness like Jane's. She'd soon lose her bloom under these conditions. I know that I was right to follow him; the weeks and months of our quarrelling have gone the way of dreams which seem so real, more real than life, and then, *puff*, they're gone.

A cut on his face has turned bad. It oozes a sickly green pus. I clean it with my rags and pick at the sores of his body. He looks like a real gypsy now, his hair long and matted about his lean face, and has a gypsy's devil-may-care acceptance of his fate. I'd like to wash his clothes and fill the house with all the perfumes of Arabia, frankincense from the Qara mountains of Dhofār, myrrh from 'Asir, balsam from the Hadhramaut.

The temple. I must set down what happened to the temple. The sands shall bury it again, leaving no trace of Sheba's glory beyond a line of crooked fingers pointing to the sky, a warning to future meddlers who arrogantly assume for themselves a power that belongs to God alone. We can create and resurrect *nothing*.

Of course it had to be. The catastrophe was inevitable from the start, nudged by man's stubborn pride which puts itself above the laws of causality. A miracle it took so long in coming.

I was there when it happened, my first appearance on site since that day he took me on the floor. I was late, I remember, and climbed on to the wall to view what progress had been made. I didn't like what I saw. The men were spread out in long lines. Some boys played near the tombs, Hamid and Mahmūd among them. They couldn't reach me now. I'd gone beyond that, into a different realm.

The temple itself had been neglected in my absence, all hands concentrated on the line of pillars at the far end. They towered above the scene. I thought I detected movement, a slight swaying in the still, desert air. Suspecting a trick of the light, I screwed up my eyes. But when I opened them again I heard an awesome rumbling in the sands and knew that the moment of reckoning had come.

The men heard it too. Dropping their tools, they turned towards the pillars, united in a common fear. Our feet stuck in clay, we watched in awed fascination as the outermost pillar shook off its flimsy support, flexing its muscles like a stone Leviathan. I felt a giddy triumph that my efforts should come to this, that I should fight the Gods on their terms and lose so gloriously.

The pillar tilted to right and left then crashed in dislocated time into the next one, and the next. Men and oxen scattered in all directions, trampling each other in their flight. The sky was filled with falling masonry, huge shafts of limestone, the heads of sacred bulls. And, as the temple sank to its knees, it roared like a wounded beast, a dragon slain, raising such a duststorm that the blackest face turned white under its covering.

And then that long last silence, the silence of the world's end, before the shouting began.

But what does it matter if the temple's gone? I've gained so much in return. We wake each morning as the sun's rays pierce the space between the houses opposite. The room glows golden yellow. I hear the guards beneath my window, disputing their spoils; and, were we free to leave, I'd not exchange these walls for anywhere.

The only drawback is the frightful food for which we'll doubtless be charged over the odds and expected to be truly thankful. The bread, when it comes, is already half-gnawed by weevils and the porridge arrives cold. It sticks in the throat like plaster of Paris and must be dislodged by great draughts of greenish water tasting of slime. I find myself consumed with longing for one of Yūsuf's interminable stews.

He's haunted by what happened at Shehārah. Often he cries in his sleep and must be roused or he will harm himself. The Imam impressed him favourably. He's neither short nor tall, a little stout, dark in complexion with a neat Arab beard. He speaks thickly, as if his tongue were too large for his mouth and has, as is usual with the Arab, a nice smile that gives his face a very pleasing expression. A pity I never made his acquaintance. I'd like to have added his name to my gallery of rogues.

'Ali's fate shall be a lesson to us. He was shot in the stomach and took a long time to die. I try to tell F. he's not to blame himself. 'Ali got his just deserts and who are we to wish it otherwise?

Once they'd bribed their way across the famous bridge of Shehārah and slithered down the slopes in the dark, taking with them as many guns as could be loaded on the backs of two weary pack animals, they stopped to rest in the plains. F. went straight to sleep but something made him stir. A sound? A chance suspicion? His low opinion of human kind? He found 'Ali with the animals, their halters ready in his hands. A thief. 'Ali was nothing better than a thief who wanted the guns for himself.

F. shot him just like that, without a word, and knelt above him as he thrashed in the dirt, dying bit by bit. F. cursed him to the end, refusing a quick bullet to the brain. So be it. Those who cheat shall be cheated in their turn. Even of life.

He has a daughter, Caroline, a plump little thing he loves more than his life. If only he'd trusted me before, I would have understood so much. For her sake alone he's slaved beneath this cruel sun, to win her a fortune and make her proud of him.

Why did he hide this from me? It changes everything. He has a wife, too, a hard-bitten woman by the sound of it, but he'll not do her down to me. She drove him away, claiming he had promised her the world then slipped his promise under his pillow and forgot about it. Her name is Ann. I see her as a dark-faced woman with his sister's eyes.

This knowledge stokes my longing. I find myself jealous of a phantom but will not cede my rightful place. We'll see who's second-best now. I've given him more than any other woman – still do. We're bound to each other for all time, bound by the things he does to me at night. He needs me every bit as much as I need him.

'We'll build our lives together,' I say. 'Caroline shall be mine. I'll give us all a home.'

He shakes his head. That beastly pride which cannot bear another's hand on his shoulder. One must have strength to take as well as give. I've told him this before. By God, I'll make him listen to me soon.

Word has reached us from the outside world. F. spoke to the guards who bring our daily bread. The Imam's revolt has collapsed and 'Izzet Pasha entered victoriously into San'ā. This news bodes ill for us. The Sharif, taking surly note of the Imam's letter, suffered our presence while he thought there was the faintest chance his overlord might call him to account. Now he considers the Turk a better paymaster and we are pawns in his rapacious game.

F. says we must leave while we can. I'd rather stay and anyway consider our chances of escape somewhat slight. F. says it isn't a question of escaping. We'll leave with the Sharif's blessing or not at all.

They tell me Michael was the only casualty, his body cut in half by the Bilqīs's stones. That's not counting four pairs of oxen and a workman who sprained an ankle as he ran away. Poor wounded Michael couldn't run. Having failed as the temple's guardian, he's better off dead.

F. reveals a new side to his character; he's become almost practical in our enforced captivity and spends a large part of his day mending things about the house, a wooden shutter here, a loose door there. I smile to myself at his new-found domesticity and catch myself thinking about the lives we might lead over there. There's Caroline to consider: I like to make plans.

Today he asked me about the nest of ants I had supposedly discovered that day I carried Sheba home. In all the excitement of the temple falling and the forging of our new life she'd quite slipped my mind. We dug her out of the floor.

'It's Sheba,' I explained, 'the Queen.'

He looked amused. 'I thought you said the temple had nothing to do with her.'

'Before I came here, yes. I know it sounds odd. But look at her. Can't you *feel* it's her? The Arabs call her Bilqīs.'

He ran his fingers down her slim cheek, and the outline of her black lips. I wanted him to do that to me.

'I've never seen anything more fair.'

'You say that to me.'

'Oh Elinor,' he said, 'there's hope for us yet.'

We put her back where she belonged, under the floor, and talked of what the world might say. He often mentions her and looks longingly at her hiding place as if he might uncover her by the act of looking alone.

Sālih it was who saved me from the men. After the pillars had toppled one by one, describing an arc against the empty sky, they turned on me like hounds at the kill, mad for my blood. I stumbled. Their weapons were crude. Hoes, picks, peasants' tools. A seething, evil mob with but one thought in its head: my blood should pay for this. They'd spike my head on Māreb's walls. Sālih sprang to my defence and rode me back to Māreb, gripping my waist and flying like the flood. We left the mob behind. I turned for one last look. Their anger had turned in on itself. And man fought man as it shall ever be, on that last day.

F. asks me a thousand questions about the temple, having developed a most gratifying curiosity. I thought he didn't care for stones. I've shown him the special notebook in which I have listed all the dry progress of my work, exact dimensions of the rooms, inscriptions, objects, conclusions and calculations. He seems to think it important. I shan't disillusion him. The truth lies elsewhere, in my head.

As for the Queen, he keeps digging her up from the floor to stare at her in wonder. I've warned him this is dangerous. If the Sharif suspects her presence, he'll snatch her from us and probably kill us too. He wants to know how she was made. What sort of men could fashion such an image. What tools they used. I answer his questions as briefly as I can, frightened of the power this new rival wields. He's still considerate but is he losing his heart?

I feel so cold. It's like the ice house at Maunton, up in the woods. I've wrapped myself in Mother's shawl and every available covering and still the cold strikes inwards. Can't he close the doors? Can't he warm me with his own heat, and rub my limbs to unfreeze the blood?

My covering was wet on waking. I've bled in the night, a thick, clotted blood that slides down my legs. The fruit of our love has seeped out of me to stain the filthy sheets. The edges of my world are blurred. I'm taken with abnormal lassitude. To drift from room to room requires an effort of superhuman will. The pen moves slowly across the page, and halts of its own accord.

I found him in another room, bent over his saddle-bags. He seemed to be preparing for a journey.

'Where are you going?' I asked, afraid. At first he ignored me. I tried to beat him with my fists. He brushed me away like a fly.

'You're sick,' he said. 'You have a fever.'

'I never felt stronger in my life. And if I *am* sick, my sickness is of a kind no mere physician can heal.'

He led me back to my room and shut me cruelly within. He would have locked it had I not snatched the key.

'Ali joined us last night. Yūsuf too. They sat cross-legged on the floor, equally glum, a couple of mourners at a wedding feast, displaced. I wanted 'Ali to tell me, in his own words, what happened. He said he'd dance for me if I would play the flute. F. stepped between us. He doesn't like me talking to 'Ali, wishing, I think, to keep me for himself. Or maybe he feels that I must never know. Doesn't he understand that, whatever happened, I have forgiven him? Hamid and Mahmūd put in a brief appearance. I shooed them away. And all the while a woman scolded in the corner like a fishwife. I'm sure it was Ann. She wasn't very pretty. At least she'd left the child behind. I can't be dealing with another's waif.

We've been through so much: we shall get through to the end. But what's he doing in the other room? I hear the sound of preparations. We can't be leaving. Not yet. I want to stay here, just the two of us.

He says he'll bring me help. That he's paid his passage with guns. What guns? What's he talking about? They took our guns away.

The house is empty. Swept and garnished too. Has Yūsuf given up his ghost? Why do I feel so strange? I can't see him any more. He doesn't answer my call. These walls are empty. She's gone, I know she's gone. My Queen. He has too. He's gone to fetch me help. I don't need help. I want him. I want him more than my life. They'll only meddle with their good intentions.

I live in a fog, I float above the ground. The light is very white. And I am ringed with dust. He'll come to fetch me soon. Take me to the other side.

Saba is green once more. The flood has rolled itself back and we have gardens again. *A fine country and a gracious Lord*. And pomegranate trees. Can't you hear the splash of fountains, feel their cool waters on your brow? We'll dance in the gardens, dance for him, a stately minuet, and walk down avenues of trees, keeping to the shady side. We shall be happy. We are happy. It's all too beautiful for words.

Why, oh why, has he abandoned me?

Part Three

JOURNEY'S END

Telegram from Dr G. A. Wendell, HBM's Vice-Consul at Hodeidah, to H.E. The Right Honourable Sir G. A. Lowther, KCMG, CB, HBM's Ambassador at Constantinople, dated 3 May 1911:

SECRET
27/E
Word reached me this morning via the local authorities at Hodeidah that a British archaeologist, Miss Elinor Jessup Grace, has been apprehended by a Turkish force at the ruins of Māreb, in Eastern Yemen, and taken captive to San'ā. In contravention of the capitulations, I have been refused permission to visit her. They suspect her of supplying guns to the rebels, which is plainly ridiculous. I met Miss Grace as she passed through Hodeidah eastwardbound, and can vouch for her character.

She must be freed at once. The Ottoman government should be asked to dismiss the Vali, Mohammed 'Ali Pasha, and to punish the other officials concerned. If the Porte refuses to listen to reason, an expeditionary force of our own might be in order. We cannot let it be known that the Turks may treat our nationals in this way with impunity. I respectfully beg that you give this letter your most urgent attention. It is hardly necessary to add that all telegraphic communication should be in cypher.

*Letter from Dr G. A. Wendell, HBM's Vice-Consul at Hodeidah
to General Sir J. A. Harris etc.; etc.; Political Resident, Aden, dated
3 May 1911:*

CONFIDENTIAL
59/M
Sir,
  I have the honour to forward herewith a copy of a
despatch which I addressed today to His Majesty's Ambassador at the Porte, reporting on the arrest and imprisonment of Miss E. J. Grace.

I have etc.;
Dr G. A. Wendell

*Telegram from H.E. The Right Honourable Sir G. A. Lowther,
KCMG, CB, Constantinople, to Sir Edward Grey, His Majesty's
Secretary of State for Foreign Affairs, dated 4 May 1911:*

SECRET
1732
Herewith enclosed telegram from HBM's Vice-Consul at
Hodeidah re. arrest and imprisonment in San'ā by Turkish
forces of British traveller, Miss Elinor Jessup Grace. Your
instructions awaited. Please note that British expeditionary
force, as proposed by Wendell, is neither practical nor
advisable. Rumours here suggest that E. Grace may indeed
have supplied guns to rebel forces. Caution advised while
Turkish authorities in San'ā attempt to reach a settlement
with Imam Yahya.

Memorandum from H. W. Harrison, Foreign Office, to Sir Richmond Ritchie, Office of Secretary of State for India in Council, Whitehall, dated 6 May 1911:

1034/11

The Under Secretary of State for Foreign Affairs presents his compliments to the Under Secretary of State for India, and begs to inform him of the arrest and imprisonment in San'ā of Miss E. J. Grace, English traveller (and, coincidentally, a second cousin of Lady Curzon). We have few details concerning the exact circumstances of the case. She was apparently engaged in archaeological excavations with the blessing of the Royal Geographical Society but not, unfortunately, the Ottoman authorities from whom permission should have been sought, notwithstanding the fact that Māreb (the presumed site of her excavations) lies somewhat outside the Ottoman sphere of influence.

I am further to state that Secretary Sir Edward Grey seeks clarification from the Political Resident at Aden how Miss Grace was able to make her way into Turkish territory. His instructions on this point were clear: HMG do not desire to encourage the exploration of Arabia, in view of the suspicions which might be aroused in the minds of Turkish officials. While short visits by British nationals to recognized places of interest are unlikely to do much harm, longer sojourns by them in places off the beaten track certainly cause suspicion and comment, especially at times of war.

Telegram from Government of Bombay to General Sir John Harris, Political Resident, Aden, dated 9 May 1911:

SECRET
939/A
The Foreign Office requests clarification of how a British

traveller, Miss E. J. Grace, successfully journeyed into Turkish Yemen, contrary to all instructions. Miss Grace apprehended by Ottomans and imprisoned at San'ā. Your considered thoughts on how this delicate situation might be handled would further be appreciated.

Telegram from General Sir John Harris, Political Resident, Aden, to Government of Bombay, dated 11 May 1911:

SECRET
No. 524
Sincerely regret embarrassment caused to HMG by capture and imprisonment of Miss E. J. Grace, globetrotter, who wilfully disregarded all advice and entreaties to abandon attempts to cross into Turkish Yemen. Action taken to prevent such an occurrence included the following:

1. Miss Grace was given all possible information (consistent with the dictates of diplomacy) concerning political situation and growing unrest within the province. Any reasonable person would have understood that a journey at such a time was, of itself, likely to provoke extreme hostility and suspicion in the minds of our allies, the Turks.

2. I personally proposed to Miss Grace that she should look elsewhere for the locus of her travels, and was led to believe that she would take up my suggestion of exploring the Barbary Coast and Morocco. I took her at her word, assuming it had some value.

3. On my express instructions, Miss Grace was shadowed by two constables of the Aden police, who filed reports each day. You will recall that on 15 December 1910, I sought clarification of my powers to apprehend persons

found acting suspiciously near the town's defences. This communication (No. 851) referred in fact to Miss Grace, who had been observed several times sketching up by the fortifications. I was preparing to have her arrested when such activity ceased, removing my grounds for complaint.

4. Again acting on my instructions, Cowasjee Dinshaw & Bros refused all her requests for a passage on one of their ships heading east for Makalla or west for the Turkish ports.

5. I let it be known in the bazaars that Miss Grace was *persona non grata* with the authorities and not to be accorded any travel facilities. In consequence, she was unable to secure transport to attempt an overland crossing into Turkish territory. Ahmed ibn Muhsin, who had helped us in the Bury case, offered Miss Grace some camels at Lahej, an offer which Miss Grace (acting on inside information?) declined. You will recall that G. W. Bury and his young companion, Gethin, wished to journey into the Yemen hinterland in 1909. It was decided to put difficulties without danger in their way. After they had made their way some fifty miles inland, said Ahmed ibn Muhsin repudiated all arrangements with the pair, who barely escaped with their lives.

6. On 23 December 1910, as noted in the weekly letter, I was informed by Miss Grace that she had decided to return home and had booked a passage on the Khedivial mail steamer as far as Suez. (Their office confirmed that this was indeed her paid-for destination.) My ADC, Captain R. Kincaid, was detailed to see her on to the ship, a duty he duly performed.

7. The first we knew of Miss Grace's duplicity was a written communication from Mr G. A. Wendell,

HBM's Vice-Consul at Hodeidah, dated 30 December
1910 but not received until 15 January 1911, to the effect
that Miss Grace had landed at Hodeidah and intended to
make her way into the interior. By this time it was too
late to prevent the inevitable débâcle. Wendell's letter
had been delayed by the outbreak of hostilities. On being
reprimanded for communicating such vital information
by letter instead of telegram Wendell begged to note that
he was following prior advice on the matter of his
expenses.

I trust the above is in order. As you can see, I did everything
in my power to stop the woman, short of incarcerating her
myself. And I would have done that if I could.

You further seek my thoughts on how to deal with this
delicate situation. First, it should be noted that, by her
actions, Miss Grace has forfeited all rights to especial consideration. The question hinges therefore on how our
interests might best be preserved. This depends on the outcome of present hostilities and what exactly took place
between Miss Grace and the leader of the rebels, Imam
Yahya. As neither question can be satisfactorily answered
in the present state of knowledge, we're somewhat in the
dark.

If the Turks remain dominant in the Yemen, we would
not wish to offend them in any way, which would rule out
of court any expeditionary or punitive force to secure our
traveller's release. If, on the other hand, Imam Yahya were
to regain the upper hand, offending the Turks would have
little material consequence. And if Miss Grace has indeed
rendered service to the Imam, it would be politic for the
British to have helped her in their turn. We must secure at all
costs a friendly power to act as a buffer state between the
British Protectorate and Ottoman territory.

Lowther's views should be sought on whether Turkish

dominance of the province is likely to continue. If pressed myself, I would hazard a guess that the Imam's revolt – like all preceding ones – will collapse, and that the Ottoman Empire will retain its present boundaries for many generations to come.

Telegram from Dr G. A. Wendell, HBM's Vice-Consul at Hodeidah, to H.E. The Right Honourable Sir G. A. Lowther, KCMG, CB, Constantinople, dated 11 May 1911:

SECRET
28/E
No reply received yet to my telegraphic communication of 3 May 1911, No. 27/E. An Englishwoman languishes in a Turkish gaol, dammit; something must be done.

Telegram from H.E. The Right Honourable Sir G. A. Lowther, KCMG, CB, Constantinople, to Sir Edward Grey, dated 13 May 1911:

SECRET
1743
Telegram received from Dr G. A. Wendell, HBM's Vice-Consul at Hodeidah, who respectfully suggests that an early reply to his communication of 3 May 1911 might be in order.

*Telegram from Sir Edward Grey to H.E. The Right Honourable Sir
G. A. Lowther, KCMG, CB, Constantinople, dated 15 May
1911:*

SECRET

2125/11

Pursuant to your communications Nos. 1732 and 1743,
herewith instructions concerning English traveller, Miss
E. J. Grace.

Authorities at Aden have confirmed that, in view of
circumstances surrounding subject's journey into Ottoman
territory, fault lies with her rather than Ottoman officials.
Furthermore, information supplied by subject's sister, to
whom Miss Grace had written secretly, suggests that her
journey was made in company of a known adventurer,
James N. Fergusson, the same Fergusson who was expelled
from Aden in 1908 following representations from the
Sultan of Lower 'Aulaqi over the sale of fifth-rate Belgian
rifles and the wrong ammunition, contrary to all regula-
tions concerning the supply of arms and ammunition to
Protectorate tribes. Accusation unproven (because Sultan
unwilling to travel to Aden to testify) but probably true.

We have no definite information about what Fergusson
might be doing in the Yemen. Calls were made on his sister,
Isobel Fergusson, and his estranged wife. The former de-
fended her brother's reputation; the latter was unable (and
unwilling?) to help. He is a most unpleasant character. At
Aden he had a peculiar habit of closeting himself with
Somali boys and, though no complaints were lodged at the
time, there was a strong impression that he was given to
Sodomy.

Situation requires delicate handling. You are instructed
to convey to the Sublime Porte a temperate though firmly-
worded protest, concentrating on conditions in which subject held captive and any possible breach of capitulations.

While Ottomans are our allies and HMG does not desire to rock the boat, British prestige in the area will suffer if it is generally known that diplomatic agreements such as capitulations can be so flagrantly breached.

Re. Miss Grace's eventual fate, you are charged to keep a watching brief. By the time a reply is received to our protest, we should know in which direction the wind of circumstance will blow. If mediator on the spot considered desirable, on no account entrust duty to Mr G. A. Wendell, who must take responsibility for allowing situation to develop in first place. Recommend close liaison with Political Resident, Aden, whose knowledge of local conditions will be invaluable.

Telegram from Dr G. A. Wendell, HBM's Vice-Consul at Hodeidah, to H.E. The Right Honourable Sir G. A. Lowther KCMG, CB, Constantinople, dated 15 May 1911:

SECRET
29/E
LOCAL AUTHORITIES GRANTED PERMISSION JOURNEY SAN'ĀWARDS. LEAVE TONIGHT. SUBSTANTIAL FINANCIAL OUTLAY REQUIRED FOR TRAVELLING EXPENSES, ARMED ESCORT, AND SAID 'PERMISSION'. TRUST HMG WILL SEE FIT TO REIMBURSE.

23 May 1911   *Bir el-'Azab, San'ā*

H.E. The Right Honourable Sir G. A. Lowther, KCMG, CB,
His Majesty's Ambassador, Constantinople

Sir,

Having accomplished my journey to San'ā in the record
time of a trifle under seven days, it is my sad duty to report
upon the condition in which I found Miss Elinor Grace
whom I was given permission to visit this morning, the day
after my arrival in the capital. The base treatment to which
she is subjected provides a clear illustration of the low
esteem in which the subjects of His Majesty the King are
held by our supposed allies, the Turks. They must be taught
a lesson, and sharply, if we're to re-establish the honour of
His name.

Miss Grace is currently held in the Citadel on the slopes of
Jebel Nuqūm in a filthy cell unfit for the meanest criminal.
Her quarters measure some eight feet by eleven (verified by
myself). They contain one Arab string bed, one chair, a
broken-down table, and scarcely room to throw a cat
besides. The window is closed with iron bars and though
her door is left open during the day, she's watched at every
turn by two armed gendarmes with fixed bayonets posted
immediately outside. The lavatory for the entire garrison, a
wretched and foul-smelling dungeon, is situated only a
dozen paces away. Its sickening smell pervades her cell
which plays host to an unkindness of vermin that makes
one's skin creep.

Please do not think I exaggerate. I've omitted certain
details in case this communication should fall into the hands
of those with weaker stomachs than yourself.

You can rest assured that I'll knock on all possible doors
to get her transferred to more suitable surroundings, pend-
ing the outcome of my efforts to secure her more permanent

release. I've requested an immediate interview with the Vali who was too busy to see me yesterday, a discourtesy I'll ignore for the present until I'm more *au fait* with the situation.

Miss Grace's state of health gives rise to even greater concern, if that were possible, than her physical surroundings. She failed to recognize me when I was shown to her cell (by 'Izzet Pasha's ADC – more about him anon). I must report that I returned the compliment. When she passed through Hodeidah some five months previously she struck me as a most resourceful woman, doughty, self-assured, a splendid battler in the rudest of health, the sort of woman on whom our Empire depends. Poking my head past her swarthy guards and, I might add, the points of their bayonets, I saw a very different specimen which led me to assume, perish the thought, there must be two Britishers in Turkish hands.

On being assured that the papers of this poor wretch confirmed her identity, I took a closer look and found myself face to face with the shadow of Miss Grace's shadow and a particularly mute one at that. She lay slumped on the string bed under a scrap of filthy blanket, her hands covered with *jurh el-Yemeni*, the characteristic Yemen ulcer, at which some flies sucked greedily.

When I'd got over my shock, I did what I could. The guards refused to shut the door while I made my examination, foolishly crediting me with supernatural powers. I do my best but cannot claim to be a conjuror. We compromised with the erection of some flimsy screens secured by the intervention of the ADC, who seems a better lot than most of his co-religionists.

The patient has suffered a severe attack of malarial fever of the remittent type. When I examined her she'd reached one of the hot stages. Her temperature was 104 degrees. I administered two Livingstone's Rousers, four tabloids of

Warburg's Tincture, a solution of ten grains of quinine, and called for quantities of cold water which we emptied over her head. A cold bath must be had as soon as possible. As the prison is poorly equipped for emergencies of this kind, the ADC offered to ask the Vali if she can be moved to the *Hukūmah* when the immediate danger is past. She needs constant nursing and I'm hopeful that the Vali will further oblige by supplying two or three of his female slaves.

As well as the fever and her pitiful sores she's badly undernourished, showing all the signs of trauma, dirt and lack of care. I can't think how she's sunk to such a low ebb. As I said, she impressed me greatly in Hodeidah and I would have considered such a transformation frankly impossible. Much in this tale requires investigation. Although her present surroundings can only add to her suffering, they're not its primary cause, and from her weakened state I judge she's been a prisoner far longer than the Turks will admit.

I stayed with her until the fever ebbed away, and I was able to leave her a mite more comfortable than before. As I took my leave, she opened her eyes and smiled at me with a look of blessed relief. 'You've come,' she said. 'I always knew you would.' At this she turned her face to the wall and sank into sleep.

That she recognized me eventually was cause for much gratification. My prognosis is that given proper care she'll recover her strength and that, providing the Turk plays fair, we need not be terminally alarmed on her account.

After I had left her sleeping like a baby, I held a frank and full discussion with Halajian Effendi, 'Izzet Pasha's ADC. The fellow enjoys a remarkable facility for languages and spoke to me in excellent English with a smattering of French that went a bit above my head. I learnt from him far more than I would have done from the Vali and am therefore pleased that I refrained from making a fuss.

The effects of Miss Grace's flight from Hodeidah I had

been able to witness at first hand. Mahir Bey, the Governor, locked up half the garrison for the unpardonable sin of having turned him into a laughing stock, a punishment he was forced to rescind when the armed uprising got out of hand and troops were required for more pressing business than defending his dignity. He has, incidentally, been replaced. The new governor, Ibrāhīm Pasha, is more incompetent than any of his predecessors during the past decade. He makes Mahir Bey appear by comparison a paragon of Turkish virtue.

She might have remained at Māreb to this day had not the Vali received a curious note. Halajian Effendi says it was written in very crude Arabic, giving details of her activities in the village. More curious still, it contained a garbled hint that her interest in archaeological sites concealed a more worldly interest in guns. Should the authorities conduct some excavations of their own in a spot indicated by the anonymous author of the note, they would understand what was meant.

An expeditionary force was sent to Māreb at once. The prisoner, already fever-stricken, was apprehended in a native house in the village where she lived in conditions of appalling squalor. They found no money on her and precious few possessions, though she'd required a full camel-train to take them from Hodeidah all those months ago. When they'd dug in the spot indicated by the note they found, as hinted, two full cases of Winchester rifles and a further case of ammunition.

The whole affair strikes me as damnably odd. Assuming that the Turks didn't pen the note themselves (and I think we can safely discount that theory because although they might stoop to the manufacture of evidence against their suspects, it seems a roundabout way to apprehend someone who has already broken their rules), I plump for the Sharif of Māreb as its most probable author. I've never met the chap myself but all those Eastern tribesmen are devilishly slippery customers. Now that it's rumoured the Turks are willing to buy the rebels' allegiance, they're buzzing around the capital like bees at a honeypot, hoping for a more generous stipend than the Imam's coffers have been able to provide. He probably put the boxes there himself.

The only flaw to this argument is that, if the Sharif wanted to prove his new loyalty to the Turks, why the devil didn't he sign the thing himself? Without his definite signature, any Tom, Dick or Harry can stake his illegitimate claim. Unless he can't write, of course.

According to Halajian Effendi, Miss Grace was shown the note by the Vali who questioned her himself as soon as she was brought to San'ā; most irregularly, I should point out, in my absence, but she told the Vali little of interest, probably because she was already too ill to do so. Anyway, he said that, when she held the note in her hands, she fainted clean away and has never since returned to proper consciousness.

My most pressing task is to settle Miss Grace into more comfortable quarters and then to get to the bottom of this baffling affair. I have proposed, first, that the Sharif of Māreb be brought to San'ā for questioning. Second, as he may prove a material witness to Miss Grace's case, I must be present at his questioning. Third and finally, I have requested permission to search Miss Grace's belongings as she must surely have kept some record, a journal, perhaps, which may shed welcome light on what exactly has taken place.

As things stand at present, we're all knocking around in the dark and the case against her looks grim. She made her journey against the express wishes of the Turkish authorities. When found at Māreb she had in her possession a letter of safe conduct signed and sealed by the Imam himself, a letter whose provenance she resolutely refuses to reveal.

Most damningly of all, she's been linked by that anonymous note to a cache of arms for which she must produce some very plausible explanation if she's to emerge with her honour intact.

I must conclude with a word about my own situation. The authorities have refused me permission to pitch my tent beyond the city walls, claiming that the chap who laid the dynamite cartridges never kept a plan. As you can imagine, he's not very popular at the moment. I am therefore forced to take lodgings in the Turkish suburb of Bir el-'Azab immediately to the west of the old city, quite comfortable apart from the bugs, which has added considerably to the expense of my journey. As I had not counted on this additional drain on my rather slim purse I may need to secure a small loan, if one is to be had in these parts.

However, now that I'm on the spot I'll be able to supply useful intelligence reports to justify the cost of my journey, notwithstanding its original cause. Cut off as we were at Hodeidah by all the recent unrest, with telegraphic communication hopelessly interrupted, intelligence was scanty and most unreliable. I may mention that the authorities at Hodeidah were not much better served in this respect and I frequently found that I knew more about the progress of 'Izzet Pasha's slow, uphill march than they did.

I'll keep you posted of each new development and trust that the arrangements I have made for the conveyance of my reports are as reliable as I have been led to believe.

I have etc.;
Dr G. A. Wendell

26 May 1911   *Bir el-ʿAzab, Sanʿā*

H.E. The Right Honourable Sir G. A. Lowther, KCMG, CB,
His Majesty's Ambassador, Constantinople

Sir,

It is my pleasure to record that at 2 p.m. yesterday Miss
Grace was transferred from the Citadel to a room in the
Hukūmah. Space was cleared for her in an antechamber
usually reserved for those wishing to petition the authorities, not much larger than her former cell but thankfully
vermin-free and smelling of nothing worse than old carpets. Her health continues to mend. The Vali has lent a
couple of slaves, who sit with her continuously, bedding
down at night on the floor, and she's able to send out for her
food. As she finds herself without funds I have guaranteed
her expenses on top of my own.

I visit her every day in the company of Halajian Effendi.
That's ʿIzzet Pasha's ADC, you will recall: a capital fellow
who has been detailed to the role of benevolent policeman as
the only reliable officer whose English is sufficiently proficient to keep track of our conversations. Their comical
fears that I may try to spring our prisoner have lessened not
one jot. We sometimes play jokes on the poor man by
speaking in low whispers, at which he has the grace to be
later amused.

Miss Grace maintains her innocence but continues to be
unhelpfully reticent. According to her version of events she
neither clapped eyes on the Imam nor buried those blasted
boxes in the sands; and, though I'm prepared to take her at
her word, she knows far more than she's willing to reveal.
Her mind has been so fogged by the fever I sometimes
wonder if she knows who she is. She bangs around like a
ghost, haunted by some weird, apocalyptic vision of the
Queen of Sheba, a sort of Second Coming, if you know

what I mean. I'm not sure I do. My wife Mary is better versed in the Scriptures than I. It's a pity she couldn't accompany me as she's frightfully brave.

In an attempt to get to the bottom of this affair as quickly as possible I tackled Miss Grace on the subject of a journal, having previously searched her belongings and found nothing beyond a few tattered clothes, a tent and odds and ends of camp equipment, a book of poems my daughter had given her and some practical handbooks on surveying which were immediately confiscated by her Turkish gaolers who fear books more than guns, especially ones they can't read.

She kept, it seems, not one record, but two: a detailed account of her excavations and a second journal of a more personal nature, a sort of jotting book, I understand.

The loss of both these journals struck her as calamitous. Without notes, her journey has shed all scientific value. She cannot re-create from memory alone the finer details of a lost world and anyway, what proof has she that what she remembers is what she saw? All her sketches have vanished too; she views them as her masterwork.

The loss of her personal journal frankly bothers me more. Without it, we've only her word to set against the evidence. Miss Grace hasn't fully comprehended its significance. When I asked for it, she became most indignant. The journal was for her eyes alone and no one, but no one, must read what it says. As the thing is lost, she'll get her way, but where the devil can it be? I'm hoping that the Sharif of Māreb will shed some light on this little mystery. Halajian Effendi assures me that he'll be here within the week and that I've been granted permission to attend his interrogation.

The Vali has so far eluded me and now I'm told he's left San'ā for a sortie against the isolated pockets of rebels based at IRRH and HEIMA. I think he wants to show 'Izzet Pasha that his inactivity during the siege of San'ā was prompted by sound policy rather than any lack of moral fibre. Word is that he will shortly be dismissed, having made as great a hash of defending San'ā as possible without actually losing the place.

In the Vali's absence I applied to see 'Izzet Pasha who has been appointed Commander-in-Chief with plenipotentiary powers; that without abrogating any of the Vali's former authority. 'Izzet Pasha denied my request on the grounds that Miss Grace's case is one for the civil authorities. I'm not sure I understand their separate responsibilities, though they're probably as much in the dark as I am. I suspect that 'Izzet Pasha wants to keep his hands clean and has decided that as the Vali was responsible for ordering Miss Grace's imprisonment in the first place, the Vali shall be left to extricate them from the whole unholy mess without too much loss of face.

Otherwise, all is quiet in the capital, metaphorically at least. We continue to receive hordes of unruly tribesmen to whom the Turks have given a total of £80,000 in San'ā alone. When not occupied with Miss Grace, I have taken the opportunity to walk around the *sūqs*, Halajian Effendi faithfully in tow, and can confirm that the recent war, with its influx of Turkish troops, has served to increase the country's general prosperity. The *sūqs* are full to bursting with a treasure trove of imported goods destined for the troops and somehow fallen by the way. This morning, for example, I saw a gramophone, several Austrian carpets and a row of spankingly new officers' uniforms for which the local Arabs will scarcely find much use unless they are given to dressing up in fancy clothes.

It's further rumoured that 'Izzet Pasha is in secret corre- spondence with the Imam at Shehārah, hoping to secure some permanent truce and the liberation of all Turkish prisoners remaining in rebel hands.

I shall communicate again as soon as we have put our questions to the Sharif of Māreb.

I have etc.;
Dr G. A. Wendell

30 May 1911   *Bir el-ʿAzab, Sanʿā*

H.E. The Right Honourable Sir G. A. Lowther, KCMG, CB,
His Majesty's Ambassador, Constantinople

Sir,

At last I have something concrete to report, though I've the deuce of a time deciding whether we're marching forwards or tripping over our heels.

The questioning of Seyyid ʿAbd er-Rahmān, Sharif of Māreb, has now taken place in the presence – required by the authorities – of both myself and Miss Grace. I had, as you know, insisted on my right to attend but Miss Grace was a very reluctant witness. He frightens her terribly, like a demon from her past. Eventually I convinced her that she alone would know if he told the truth, rather than some half-baked notions of his own. My desire for certainty overruled any doubts I entertained as to her medical fitness for the ordeal. I need not have worried: she's constitutionally as strong as an ox.

The Sharif's questioning took place in the *Hukūmah*. Instead of being directed by the simplest route, Miss Grace, Halajian Effendi and myself were led out of a side door, round the building to the main courtyard and in again through the front door, a comedy performed entirely for the amusement of a noisy throng of onlookers, curious rather than hostile. Halajian Effendi whispered to me that they had gathered in the expectation that we were to be publicly hanged, one of his little jokes, I think, to repay mine.

Once back inside the *Hukūmah*, we were escorted to the august presence of the *Qādhi*, a man as solemn as Moses, wearing a large white puffball on his head. He sat behind a rickety table laden with books and filled me with the fear of God. Miss Grace, bless her soul, managed to smile at him.

The courtroom bustled and chattered around us. When we were seated, the *Qādhi* thundered for silence, a request everyone ignored, and the witness was ordered to stand, a fawning, unscrupulous ruffian if ever I saw one.

To my surprise, instead of putting the man sharply through his paces the clerk of the court proceeded to read out a most preposterous statement in which the Sharif of Māreb laid claim to a colossal sum of money owed to him, he said, by the Feringhee Miss Grace. I was so taken aback, thinking we were there to interrogate him rather than the other way round, that I failed to make proper notes but, if my memory serves me well, the sums requested were intended to cover the following:

(a) wages for one foreman, thirty-one men and fifty-three boys, all employed to work on Miss Grace's excavations for a period of some two months, during which time they'd been paid by the Sharif himself on the understanding that Miss Grace would settle her account when the excavations were complete;

(b) the services of three bodyguards, necessary to protect Miss Grace from the anger of her workforce who had discovered they were being cheated of a large portion of the wages graciously disbursed from his own coffers;

(c) reparations requested by the family of Sakhr ibn Khālid who had come to an untimely end owing to Miss

Grace's dilatoriness on site and whom he, the Sharif, loved better than a brother;

(d) accommodation, food and the like provided for Miss Grace and her party in the village and not yet paid for;

(e) the cost of priceless treasures removed illegally from the site; alternatively, return of said treasures, in which case the sum would be reduced to punitive damages for the inconvenience caused.

On top of everything else, Miss Grace has been accused of manslaughter and common thievery. I was able to put a stop to these ridiculous proceedings at once by pointing out to the *Qādhi* that, as a foreigner covered by the capitulations, Miss Grace fell into my jurisdiction, not his, and that I would investigate the Sharif's claims with all due process of law and let him know my verdict as soon as it was reached. Miss Grace, I have to say, looked a little disappointed at this, and the *Qādhi* simply nonplussed. He said he would defer to the Vali who, being out of town, couldn't rule on the matter immediately, so we all went home by the same roundabout route as before.

The two parties remain at loggerheads. As far as Miss Grace is concerned, the only truth spoken by the Sharif concerns the cheating of her men (it goes without saying that she wasn't herself responsible), while the Sharif, whom I interviewed shortly afterwards, sticks to his guns and says he can call witnesses to prove his case. By and by I asked him about the anonymous note linking Miss Grace to the arms cache. I have to say he looked genuinely surprised, even angry, and swore most brutally at the Christian's ways. I'll let him calm down a bit before I tackle him again.

This case drags on interminably; I wonder how affairs progress at Hodeidah from whence no word since I set out for San'ā. I would like to think that when the Vali returns we'll be granted permission to leave but my optimism wears a little thin and a punitive force sent up from Aden may yet be needed to pull us out of the bag.

I have etc.;
Dr G. A. Wendell

1 June 1911   *Bir el-'Azab, San'ā*

H.E. The Right Honourable Sir G. A. Lowther, KCMG, CB,
His Majesty's Ambassador, Constantinople

Sir,

My wife forwarded your telegram, which arrived first thing this morning along with several other papers. I note its contents and regret most deeply that I cannot comply with its principal command.

You say that I must leave San'ā at once, with or without Miss Grace. I beg most respectfully to point out that by this action we would throw her to the wolves. The humble soldier in the field must at times be allowed to apply his own discretion, having a better measure of his enemy than the general who remains further afield. I am that humble soldier, sir, and hope you will not think too badly of me if I remain in the capital until she is set free. Having helped her into this mess, I cannot abandon her now.

You have further requested information about a certain James Fergusson whom you understand to have travelled with Miss Grace, a request with which I can more easily comply. I met the man myself when they passed through Hodeidah, though his somewhat murky past was only later communicated to me by Aden who wanted to know if I'd come across any stray Europeans knocking about the Tihā-mah. From the information supplied it was obvious that Fergusson was the chap in mind.

Shortly after Miss Grace's (lone) arrival in the port, he

had accosted me in the *sūqs* and introduced himself as the woman's sweetheart. An affair of the heart, I thought, that probably ran counter to the wishes of her family because he insisted I should mention our encounter to no one, not even Miss Grace whom he wanted to surprise.

With hindsight, I was foolish to take him at his word but he seemed a proper sahib, a well-plucked one too, and I frankly sympathized with his expressed desire for a spot of adventure in the interior. It further seemed too private and unimportant a matter to communicate to Your Excellency. If my judgement was wanting at least my intentions were good.

They travelled together for a period of roughly four weeks, after which their ways parted and Miss Grace continued alone to Māreb. He wrote to me, you see, from Hajjah, saying that circumstances had forced them apart and commending her to my long-distance care. I continued to think well of the man until Kincaid at Aden got in touch and I was struck by the full folly of my ways. You can imagine how I felt, having helped Miss Grace to step inside the lion's den.

Now that his existence is known to you, I can reveal that all fingers (except Miss Grace's) point to the likelihood of his having spent at least some time with her at Māreb. The Sharif intimated as much: he said Miss Grace was joined by a tall, brutish fellow with a penchant for Arab boys who went by the name of Abu Nawār which, according to Kincaid's letter, is an habitual alias of his.

You might not have come across the Nawār. A tribe of gypsies, like the Sulubba, they ply their trade as smiths, tinkers, carpenters and cattle surgeons to the Bedu. They're said to eat carrion and vermin such as hedgehogs. An odd choice of alias, I think you'd agree.

I omitted all mention of him from my earlier reports as I wanted to be sure of my facts. Now I can safely say that if we're looking for a gun-runner Fergusson's our man.

Unfortunately for us, however, Miss Grace flatly denies that he ever caught up with her again. 'Oh no,' she said, when told of my conversation with the Sharif. 'We travelled only as far as Hajjah and then a quarrel forced us apart.' I asked her what the quarrel concerned. She implied it was impertinent to ask. Damned difficult, as you can see.

I tried as delicately as I could to establish the true nature of their relations, hinting even at what Fergusson had told me at Hodeidah. 'I wasn't his sweetheart then,' she said, smiling like an angel. 'We were only good friends.' I must say I'd like to knock some sense into her. Unless she admits that he joined her at Māreb, we'll never succeed in clearing her name.

The air up here is so thin it's obviously affected her brain. I've offered her books which she doesn't want to read. I've tried to discuss the latest news, but politics leaves her cold and she doesn't care a fig for Women's Suffrage. To keep up her spirits, I gave her a parcel from home, addressed to her at the Consulate, which my wife sent up. Among other things, it contained a number of evening dresses at which she glanced idly and bequeathed to the two delighted slave girls who, apart from my visits, provide her only company and I must say it shows. She's let them dye her hands with henna, one spotted orange, the other crudely zigzagged. It makes me bleed to see the change that has come over her.

You must understand, sir, why I cannot leave her now. I place my future in your hands and seek your pardon for the past. Although my presence here is irregular, I shall continue to keep you informed.

With truth and great respect,
Notwithstanding our difference of view,
I remain,
The humblest of your servants,
Dr G. A. Wendell

3 *June 1911*   *Bir el-'Azab, San'ā*

H.E. The Right Honourable Sir G. A. Lowther, KCMG, CB,
His Majesty's Ambassador, Constantinople

Sir,

The Vali has returned to San'ā, having failed to find the
enemy. In pressing my request for an interview I am passed
between the Vali and the General like a shuttlecock. 'Izzet
Pasha continues to assert that Miss Grace's case concerns the
civil authorities. The Vali is equally adamant that, as
the chief charge against her is that of supplying guns to the
insurgents, the matter is one for the military. I don't care
who sees us as long as someone does, and soon.

We've heard no more about the Sharif's claim which is
just as well, as neither Miss Grace nor I have funds to meet
the barest fraction of it. He has, I believe, returned to Māreb
with a stipend and a Turkish flag.

I have etc.;
Dr G. A. Wendell

7 *June 1911*   *Bir el-'Azab, San'ā*

H.E. The Right Honourable Sir G. A. Lowther, KCMG, CB,
His Majesty's Ambassador, Constantinople

Sir,

It is with a heavy heart that I record our interview with
the authorities finally took place on 5 June 1911 at the Vali's
residence on the Mīdān esh-Sherara. We're free to leave
San'ā as soon as an escort can be arranged. Although I've
achieved my goal in coming to the capital you will doubtless feel that the price exacted has been unduly high.

I would have moved heaven and earth to prevent such a
conclusion. May I point out in Miss Grace's defence that

she's not the woman she was. Not only has she suffered much but the fever has clouded her normally clear head. In her present state of mind a court of law would not, I think, hold her responsible for anything. I'm not a legal brain, of course, but you've only to look at her to absolve her of blame. How I rail at Turkish trickery, which brings a man to his knees then kicks him full and squarely in the stomach.

As you will wish to know exactly what passed between us, I append the full record of the meeting between Miss Grace, myself and the two Turkish chiefs, a compromise solution proposed by myself to their problem of overlapping jurisdictions. My fault, I'm afraid. I should have held out for a meeting with the Vali alone: he's far too nice a man to take advantage of another's misfortune. Any gaps in my notes I've filled with the help of Halajian Effendi, who acted as official interpreter, though we mostly spoke French.

You won't like what follows, sir. Neither do I. We've landed in the devil of a mess from which only a great deal of diplomacy, and a few well-timed overtures to the Turks, can hope to extricate ourselves. Your chaps will have a better idea than I of how this might be done.

NOTES OF MEETING THAT TOOK PLACE ON MONDAY, 5 JUNE 1911, P.M., AT THE VALI'S RESIDENCY, SAN'Ā

PRESENT: General 'Izzet Pasha, Commander-in-Chief of the Turkish forces
Mohammed 'Ali Pasha, Vali of el-Yemen
Miss Elinor Jessup Grace, British traveller and archaeologist
Dr George Alfred Wendell, HBM's Vice-Consul, Hodeidah
Halajian Effendi, ADC to General 'Izzet Pasha

Notes prepared by Dr G. A. Wendell in consultation with the last named above.

At approximately 1 p.m., Halajian Effendi arrived at the *Hukūmah* with an armed guard to escort Miss Elinor Grace and myself through the old city to the Vali's Residency, a pleasant, rambling building set in fine gardens to the right of the open space known as the Mīdān esh-Sherara. Our walk through the town passed off without incident beyond the usual crowds.

On being told to wait in a shabby antechamber on the first floor, cluttered with poor imitation French furniture, I attempted to put Miss Grace at her ease. Not that she was agitated. Far from it. What worried me most was her abnormal calm. She had at least hid her bizarrely patterned hands in a pair of white gloves.

After the necessary wait, the massive wooden doors were thrown open and we were ushered into a chamber the size of a ballroom, at the far end of which were seated two Turkish gentlemen, Tweedledum and Tweedledee, their chests blazing with medals. To the gentleman on the right (General 'Izzet Pasha) I took an instant dislike. He eyed us like a cold fish as we made our way across the dance floor, in direct contrast to the Vali who was manners personified and reminded Miss Grace of an earlier encounter in Syria. She nodded curtly and gave him the ghost of a smile. From her manner I knew we were in for a pretty rough ride.

The General, soon tiring of Mohammed 'Ali Pasha's more measured pleasantries, smiled at Miss Grace like a lizard. 'I would like to know,' he said, 'why you came to our land.'

She turned on him her most practised smile. 'Your land?' she asked. 'You mean el-Yemen?'

'Of course I mean el-Yemen.'

'That must be obvious, surely. You found me at Māreb.'

'Nothing is obvious at a time of war.'

'Oh, that business. There wasn't a war going on, when I came. I wanted to examine the ruins at Māreb. Since

Glaser's visit, we haven't heard whisper from the place. He brought back, you may recall, literally hundreds of inscriptions. I hoped to add to his collection. It's most remarkable, you see. Glaser's fragments had some surprising gaps. He found no law codes, no epics, no myths, a single poem the only evidence of any literature. Imagine that. Glaser did, of course, bring back plenty of lists.'

'I would be grateful if you would answer my question.'

'I'm trying to, sir. I'm a scholar, you see. These things are important to me. At least, they were when I came. It's very hard, don't you think, to remember exactly how one felt, at any particular time?'

'I put it to you, Miss Grace, that you came as a British spy.'

She gave him a look of pure exasperation, such as one reserves for the antics of a tiresome child. 'I can vouch for that, sir,' I put in quickly. 'Miss Grace is not, and never has been, in the employ of His Majesty's Government. I may go so far as to say that they didn't approve of her journey. I believe the authorities at Aden tried to stop her coming in.'

'Nonsense,' said Miss Grace. 'General Sir John Harris is a very dear friend. He's the Political Resident at Aden, you know.'

'He might be a friend, Miss Grace,' I said in low voice, 'but he didn't *approve*.'

She chose to ignore my hint. 'I don't care tuppence whether he approved or not. He did seem rather keen on Morocco. These military men . . . They never quite grasp the point.'

The Vali stepped quickly into the awkward silence that ensued. 'Did you find what you were seeking at Māreb?' he asked, blinking benevolently in the sunlight.

Miss Grace looked towards the window with its view of the wide-open space. All was peaceful. One could see the tops of the trees in the Vali's garden. I remember feeling heartily relieved to have escaped the noisy babel of the city. Without looking at him, she said quietly, 'I did.'

The General rattled his medals impatiently. 'You will tell me more about your journey.'

'Ask what you will.'

'You travelled alone?'

'I always travel alone. You must know, sir,' she said to the Vali, 'my reputation on that score.'

He nodded. I wondered which was worse: to let her hang herself with this confounded claim, or to throw in my spanner and have her word denied.

'Without servants?' went on the General, before I had time to decide.

'Oh, I always take plenty of those. This time I had only one. His name was Yūsuf. I can recommend him to you. He cooks very good stews.'

'Where is he now?'

She looked around her chair, surprised. 'I really don't know. I last remember him at Māreb. He came to a gathering, some feast or other. It gets rather confused after that. He wasn't very well, you see. Did he die?'

'Miss Grace has suffered an attack of malaria,' I said. 'She wasn't *compos mentis* by the end.' At this she glowered at me.

'So you travelled alone. With a servant boy.'

'A man.'

'Can you tell me your route?'

'Let's not bother with that. I don't want to get anyone into trouble. We stopped for a time in a village near Menākhah. They didn't want us to stay but couldn't let us loose in all that beastly war. Anyway, we eventually made our escape. We travelled north . . . '

'To Shehārah?'

'I never reached Shehārah; then east, skirting the plains of 'Amrān. I didn't keep a record of that part of the journey.

The country was pretty monotonous. We travelled as fast as we could.'

'You carried, I understand, a letter from Imam Yahya, guaranteeing your safe conduct through the tribes?'

'Correct.'

'This is the letter?' 'Izzet Pasha waved his hand at Halajian Effendi, who produced a document stout as a barrister's brief, that bore a most impressive seal. 'Read it, if you please.'

Halajian Effendi read it first in faultness Arabic, and then gave an extempore rendition in French. It went as follows:

I commend unto your hands, oh friends, the bearer of this letter. The Prophet, may the blessings of God be upon him, his relations and friends, said, 'Love God for the prosperity he has bestowed on you; love me for the love of God; and love my descendants for my love.'

And He also said, 'I shall live with you after my death, and so shall the Holy Book of God and my own relations which, if you adhere to and observe, you shall never go astray, but come instead to the fountain which is in paradise.'

As you well know, I am descended from the Prophet's relations. Do therefore as I ask, oh friends, and you shall get your reward. For these are evil times. The Turks have clothed themselves in the dress of cruelty amongst the inhabitants of this world and adorned themselves with ornaments of sin and aggression. When we called upon them to observe the law, they bit their fingers with disappointment and bent their heads downward in a supercilious manner. Now the sword is drawn from its scabbard. God willing, it shall produce on them distress and gloom.

It has been said by the Arab poet, 'He who does not tend his cistern will find it demolished.' And then again,

'He who does not repel force will himself be repelled.'
Now with our friends, may God add to their perfections,
we shall make *jihād* trusting in the worshipped God.

Imam Yahya ibn Mohammed el-Mansūr ibn Yahya,
Commander of the Faithful who trusts in God the Lord of
the Two Worlds.

I spotted it at once, of course. In a proper court of law, this
blasted letter, which has caused us no end of trouble, would
prove nothing. It wasn't made out in Miss Grace's name,
you see. She might have found it upon a stone, for all we
know. Certainly she made use of it – who wouldn't? – But
it wasn't, by a long chalk, what one would call conclusive
evidence.

I said as much to the General who puffed like a discon-
certed toad, then turned on Halajian Effendi whom he
boxed verbally about the ears. The Vali, delighted by the
other's discomfiture, continued to smile at us.

To press our advantage I said to Miss Grace, 'It's clear the
letter wasn't meant for you.'

'How do you know?' she snapped.

'The Imam appears to suggest that whoever carries the
letter is about to render him some service. In connection
with his . . . his quarrel, let's say, with the authorities.'

'That's one way of reading it.'

'But you never met the Imam, did you? We have your
sworn statement to that effect.'

'I never met him, no.'

'May I respectfully suggest, Miss Grace, that the letter
was written for *someone else*.'

Silence reigned as all eyes turned to her. She lowered her
glance. Below the calm exterior, a furnace burned. A vein in
her neck pulsed wildly. If I could only sit in her place and
give them the answers required, we would be off the hook
before you could say James Fergusson. The Vali coughed.

The sound of raised voices outside the door. Someone said, in Turkish, 'You cannot enter now.'

Miss Grace raised her head and looked me grimly in the eye. With all my might I willed her to tell the truth. 'Pray give us your views, my dear, on whom that someone else might be.'

She would have spoken there and then, I swear it, had not the door swung open to admit a boy of about twelve pursued by a large, oily Negro. The boy had long, flaxen hair and wore the uniform of a palace guard, a cut-down dagger stuffed into his waistband. He ran straight between the legs of the Vali who smiled at him, his son, and waved the Negro away.

Miss Grace shook herself, as if she had suddenly woken up, and threw the ball back at me. 'I haven't the faintest idea,' she said. 'I said I travelled alone. Perhaps you can enlighten us, Dr Wendell. You seem to know my business better than I.'

I felt damned uncomfortable to be poked at like a gangly fly.

The Vali spoke indulgently to the boy tucked between his knees.

'Izzet Pasha said, 'We'll leave the Imam's letter for the moment. I want you to tell me what happened, at Māreb. We've received all manner of complaints. You are, I understand, an archaeologist?' He spoke the word with distaste.

'Among other things, yes.'

'Of some repute.'

She smiled nicely.

'Then how do you explain what went wrong? The Sharif reports that your work on the greatest of the temples resulted in its entire demolition.'

She turned a little red. This was news to me. I'd heard about an accident, but nothing on this scale. 'Is that right, Miss Grace?' I asked.

She nodded. 'It wasn't my fault though I was, I suppose, in charge. The men were working in the wrong place. I told them not to but . . . no one listened.'

'A man was killed,' said the General.

'Yes, my friend, Michael.'

'Michael?'

Halajian Effendi looked at some papers. 'His name was Sakhr ibn Khālid.'

'I called him Michael. After the archangel. I should have called him Gabriel. He was always bringing me messages, you see.'

The General raised his eyebrows. I probably raised mine.

'Gabriel, the messenger. In the *Qur'ān*. You've read it, I suppose?'

The General looked shocked. Convinced that this line of questioning would get us nowhere, I slipped in a few practical questions of my own about her excavations, which need not concern us here. This excavating business seems a dull and pretty dry affair to me. Despite her missing records she retained a fine grasp of detail but I couldn't help contrasting her present manner with the early fires at Hodeidah.

The Vali translated occasionally for the benefit of his son who watched the foreign woman, open-mouthed. The General looked bored and, when she broached the subject of how she had examined some desiccated goat droppings for whatever light they could shed on the vexed question of the temple's dating, he broke in brutally and asked about the guns.

'The guns?' she enquired, faltering for the first time. 'What guns?'

'The ones you buried in the sands.'

'I didn't. I swear it.'

'We've reason to believe that you put them there your-self.'

'But how? They're not my guns.'

'There was that business of the note,' I said, squeezing her hand.

She looked at me, alarmed. 'What note? What are you talking about?'

'You must remember, Miss Grace,' I said. 'The note that led them to you. We've spoken of it before. I think they showed it to you.'

'Oh no, they didn't,' she replied, emphatically shaking her head. 'I don't remember any note. The Imam's letter, yes, but nothing else. Who wrote it?'

'We don't know. That's the point. It bore no signature.'

'A note without a signature? How beastly odd.' Her laugh was hollow like an empty jar. As a medical man, I should have brought the proceedings to an immediate halt. The signs were clear as day. She was too weak to take further strain.

'I've got it here,' said Halajian Effendi, rustling again through his papers. She looked ready to run away.

I snatched it from him and glanced quickly at the crudely-formed script. Without measuring the consequences, I gasped aloud. 'My God,' I said, 'I recognize the hand. Upon my soul, it's James Fergusson's.'

She screamed and jumped to her feet. The Vali clapped his hands. Several Negro slaves grasped her roughly by the arms. I was too astonished by my revelation to pay much attention to the poor patient. I remember repeating several times, *James Fergusson, who the devil would have thought it?* which only added to the general confusion. Miss Grace screamed at every mention of his name and then, eluding the slaves, ran over to me and pummelled my chest like a punchbag.

'It wasn't James,' she shouted. 'Say it wasn't him. I'll do whatever they ask. They can hang me if they like, but say it wasn't him. He wasn't there, truthfully. He'd gone to fetch me help. I'd fallen sick. I couldn't cure myself. You know it wasn't him. He'd never, on his life, abandon me.' She grasped at my knees. It was horrible to see the state to which she'd sunk.

The slaves picked her bodily from the floor and carried her kicking and screaming to a chair. I cursed myself for having left my medical kit at home. The General pushed me towards the window, saying Miss Grace would soon calm down. She was merely hysterical. I know these chaps have several wives, but even so he seemed a callous sort.

At the window 'Izzet Pasha questioned me about this fellow Fergusson. The patient's screams grew fainter. Having let the blasted cat out of the bag, I decided quickly to tell him all I knew, a sort of betrayal for a better cause. And quietly done. She mustn't overhear or the screaming would start all over again.

'He's another spy for the British Government?'

'Good God, no. Aden would clap him in gaol, if they could.'

'You're sure the writing is his?'

'Positive. He wrote to me, you see.'

'In Arabic?' The General has a way of screwing up his brow in disbelief.

'Not the letter, of course. But he'd written my name on the outside and the Consulate's address. In case it went missing, I suppose. I've got the letter at my lodgings. We can compare the two, if you like, but I'm as certain as can be that the hand is the same.'

The General pondered this information. Outside, on the Mīdān esh-Sherara, a straggling band of soldiers drilled up and down. They looked better dressed than formerly and I can report that all wore boots.

'What connects Miss Grace to this Mr . . . Fergusson?'

'I wish I knew,' I replied miserably.

'They travelled together, I presume?'

I had to come clean. I explained that the pair had set out together from Hodeidah but that after a time she had continued alone.

'That's why he wrote to me, you see. He asked me to keep an eye on her.'

'Where did he go after that?'

'He gave me no hint. I've always assumed he went on to Shehārah.'

'With your Government's support?'

'No. In helping them to escape from Hodeidah, I acted off my own bat. The General was furious when he found out. He wanted my scalp; probably still does.'

'And then he joined her later at Māreb?'

'I think so, yes. She won't admit as much but someone did. It must have been him. Look here,' I said, 'I didn't realize the affair was political.'

'Everything with the British is political. You must know that, Dr Wendell.'

'I thought it was a question of the heart.'

We looked over at poor Miss Grace. She sat pinned to a chair, her fires snuffed, fanned by the Vali with a sheaf of papers that included Fergusson's note.

'She lied to me,' said the General. 'You did too. That changes everything.' He didn't explain how, and I felt I'd forfeited the right to ask. He'd got us over a barrel.

The General walked slowly across the room and stood for a time looking down at her. She kept her eyes on the floor. Very deliberately, he reached for her chin, tilting her face sharply to the light. Her eyes were dull with misery. 'He's caught and plucked you, my little sparrow,' he said with a smile.

She jerked her head and spat. His hand recoiled. He looked for a second as if he might strike her. I ran to her side, ready to defend her if he so much as lifted a finger.

He wiped the spittle from his face. And then his smile

grew, the smile of one accustomed to conquest. A smile that encompassed our complete humiliations, for we were both, in a manner of speaking, brought to our knees, Miss Grace for her sins and I for my disgrace.

We had to act quickly. I tackled the Vali as the more humane of the pair and asked if a room might be found for her in his house. The shock had been too great to let us move her. The good man agreed at once and despatched one of his slaves with orders to prepare a room in the women's quarters, the best room. He continued to fan her with his papers and I tried to indicate – without her seeing – that Fergusson's note was plainly visible on top. I should have whisked her away before the final damage was done.

The General locked her in his glance.

She sat very straight, a slave crouched on either side of her.

His smile held.

Looking into his eyes, she frowned, as if attempting to read their meaning and discover some hope for herself.

These signs took place without my cognizance but Hala-jian Effendi confirmed afterwards that she had smiled too and sighed, more in relief than desperation.

The Vali and I continued to make our arrangements, oblivious to the currents passing under our noses.

'You want to know what happened?' she said to the General.

Her voice gave me the shivers. It came from deep underground, deeper even than the tombs. Slow, disembodied. It turned my blood cold.

'Miss Grace,' I said, 'I beg you not to speak.' The General pushed me away.

'Yes,' she said, ignoring my intervention, 'we took the guns to the rebels at Shehārah, myself and Mr Fergusson. Child's play, really. You were all far too busy killing each other to bother about us. And yes, if you must know, we had the full support of my Government. We did it for King and country and a fair-sized reward. The guns we brought in from Aden, courtesy of the Sultan of Lahej.'

'What nonsense,' I interposed. 'The Sultan is our friend. Our best friend in the Protectorate.'

'Shut up,' said the General.

'We had an accomplice. His name was 'Ali ibn 'Abdullah, a rascally sort, one of the Imam's retinue. He'd worked previously in Aden for a Captain Kincaid. You may have heard of him. Right-hand man to the Resident. You should talk to him one of these days. He has some very interesting notions. He thinks your time is done. That your Empire is founded on sand and soon will crumble away. He's a man of the future, is Captain Kincaid. I'm sure he's absolutely right.

'With the Captain's connivance, 'Ali arranged the Imam's letter for us. I can talk of him now, because he's dead. We shot him, you see. After we'd come down from the mountain. He'd overreached himself and tried to trick us of the rebels' reward. Greed works like poison, don't you think? He gave us no choice. And after we'd shot him my friend lay low for a time, a man marked by blood. I continued alone into the desert but not for long, you understand. My friend soon joined me there. We lived side by side, in perfect harmony. We worked together on the temple.'

She frowned. 'It did go rather wrong, I'm afraid. I'm sad about that, it was a very special temple, to me, but it's . . . understandable, you must grant me that. My heart was otherwise engaged.'

'And the note, Miss Grace?' asked the General.

'Ah yes, the note . . . ' There was a look of triumph in her eyes. 'That was our only mistake. We planned it together, you see. I'd fallen sick, and needed a doctor, urgently. You have the only doctors, sir. You had to come to my aid. That business of the guns . . . We'd kept them as a form of surety, suspecting that the double agent would double-cross again. He meant to point a finger at the Sharif of Māreb, who cheated us and bled us dry. The letter should have said the guns were his. I never saw it, myself. By then I was much too ill. He must have penned it in a hurry, before making his escape.'

The General screwed up his brow. 'Your friend, this Mr Fergusson, where is he now?'

She shrugged. 'I've told you everything I know.'

I remember shaking my head like a wet dog, unable to believe my ears.

The General turned on his heels. The time was approximately half-past three. We heard the muezzin's chant arise from scattered points within the city. '*Allah akbar*', God is the greater.

At the door the General said, 'I'll have a statement prepared. As soon as she has signed, you're free to go.'

And that, sir, is what happened. I was a witness to her signing, having attempted most earnestly to change her mind. As she was lodged with the women, my way was barred. I saw her only once, before the signing. She seemed composed and physically in shape but, as for her mind, well, her grasp of reality had gone. When I painted the dire international consequences of her 'confession', she pushed the blame on to poor Captain Kincaid, saying he should have thought of that before. If one holds to unconventional opinions, one must be prepared to have them discussed. She sticks to a story like a limpet and will not be budged.

The Vali having washed his hands of us, I requested and was granted an audience with General 'Izzet Pasha, who was coldly polite. I like him no better than before and trust him far less. He says, small comfort, that he'll use her confession only if forced to do so.

———

'It's always useful, don't you think,' he confided, 'to have compromised one's friends?'

We leave, I hope, tomorrow. Miss Grace shall stay with me at the Consulate, until she has fully recovered from her ordeal. I expect they'll want to see her at Aden, on her way home. I hope they'll treat her gently, for all the trouble she has caused.

Finally, sir, may I confirm my earlier reports that 'Izzet Pasha has indeed entered into correspondence with the Imam, a fact he confirmed to me personally. A deal is being struck which strips the Imam of his titles and all claim to the Caliphate. He must release all Turkish prisoners and some four hundred Arab hostages, the fulcrum of his authority over the highland tribes. In return, he shall receive a subsidy of something like £25,000 from the revenues of the *vilayet* and the *Sheriah*, or Islamic law, will be substituted in the highland districts for the judicial code at present pertaining.

Since the collapse of his revolt, IMAM YAHYA has lost the sympathy of an influential section of his co-religionists. There are signs of alienation from him, of open revolt against his authority. This factor has played an important part in the present negotiations, inducing him to make the best of any bargain offered by the Turks.

I'm sorry, sir, I really am,
Dr G. A. Wendell

23 June 1911   *British Vice-Consulate,*
Hodeidah & Camaran

H.E. The Right Honourable Sir G. A. Lowther, KCMG, CB,
His Majesty's Ambassador, Constantinople

Sir,
   I beg to acknowledge receipt of your telegram No. 2003,

which my wife handed to me early this morning when we finally arrived home. I shall present myself at the India Office in London as soon as a passage may be arranged. Although it would make sense to take Miss Grace with me, I regret that her fever has recurred. As she's flat on her back my good wife refuses to let her travel again until she's quite on the mend.

Our journey to the coast took nearly two weeks. The road is ravaged by war and we saw signs of much desolation. The Mudir of Police, no less, accompanied us, and seven armed guards whom I was forced to pay out of my own pocket. As you see, the expenses of my journey have continued to mount. I'll let them have a full account in London to prevent any difficulties arising over payment of the same.

Notwithstanding the Mudir's rank, no arrangements had been made for us on the way down. We stayed at flea-bitten rest houses and subsisted mostly on a diet of tinned sardines.

Halajian Effendi came to see us off at the Bāb el-Yahūd. I was sorry to see him go. He's rendered every possible service: a minor medal wouldn't go amiss. The General was notable by his absence. At the last minute he sent word that he was 'too busy' to bid us goodbye. Good riddance, I'd say. He's packed the Vali off to JEIZĀN where more trouble brews, this time a revolt under SEYYID MOHAMMED IDRĪSI from 'Asīr. Time alone will help to clear the storms overclouding the political horizon in this eventful corner of the Ottoman Empire. We have the devil of a job keeping up with events.

Miss Grace made a very silent companion, quite blind to the rare and extraordinary sights of her journey. We saw some splendid specimens, including a bird of paradise fly catcher, and, wonder of wonders, a small herd of ibex in the highlands. Do you know, I don't think she even noticed them? She kept her eyes on the road and from her hazy look

I guessed that she were somewhere else across the mountains, far away. I tried to chivvy her along but decided in the end it was kindest to let her be.

The fever struck again shortly before we dropped into the plains. She had to be carried the last thirty miles on a stretcher and fearing the worst I promised the bearers double rations should their cargo reach Hodeidah alive. We passed the Turkish fort at 3 a.m. this morning, trotting briskly in the moonlight, and though by then she'd lost consciousness the men had clearly earned their reward.

It's just as well she wasn't entirely of the living. Among the Reuters telegrams that awaited me was a report, filed in Cairo, to the effect that a certain James Fergusson was returning home after a most illustrious and illuminating expedition to Māreb, legendary home of the Queen of Sheba, from whence he brought a quantity of drawings, plans, inscriptions, and – the devil take the man – a likeness of the Queen herself. I think he had her head.

You may have seen the telegram. Fergusson took a bow as the daring Scottish traveller, well-versed in native ways and modes of thought, and drew much credit for having lifted a corner of the veil that hangs over Darkest Arabia.

The fellow's effrontery leaves me gasping for breath. We'll keep the news from Miss Grace as long as we dare but she's bound to find out in the end. I'd be grateful for any advice on how we might have the man cashiered. The ordinary punishments are far too good for a blackguard like him.

I understand from your telegram that you have also been recalled to HQ. I hope you'll put in a good word for me, sir. I did what I could, like a good soldier. You know that better than most.

I have etc.;
Dr G. A. Wendell

★

14 December 1911   *Maunton Grange, Otterburn,*
Northumberland

Dear Doctor Wendell,

I believe that certain episodes in life should, like stories, have a decent end. A time must come when one decides to draw the line; to tot up the sum of one's suffering before writing the episode into the fixed ledger of one's experience, a sort of spiritual balance sheet, if you like, recorded with the financier's dispassionate eye. That's why I'm writing this to you, dear Doctor, knowing you are the one person who may possibly understand.

I was so very sad not to see you when you called at Maunton. They didn't tell me about your visit until several weeks afterwards, suspecting that had I known you were in the house I would have risen from my bed and walked, however ill I was at the time. They meant it for the best but, oh, how sad it made me feel. We could have shared so much. You knew him, you see, and though I doubt whether your opinion of him is very high we could at least have talked, you and I, and talking might have helped me to forget.

Besides, I would so like to have caught up with your news. Were they very hard on you in London? I'd have put in a good word for you if anyone had asked: you of all people know how much I stand in your debt. Without your courageous help I would languish to this day in Sanʿā, swept under Turkish carpets by those in whom I had foolishly put my trust. It's unpleasant to discover that saving national face counts for more than preserving the lives of us more simple folk.

But do not mistake my intentions, dear Doctor. I've no mind to mope about like poor old Yūsuf, bewailing my fate and the bland treachery of those at the helm. One must assume responsibility for failure as well as success.

And so I sit here in my room, bracing myself for the hard task ahead. Keeping accounts has always struck me as a necessary chore and I'm as well prepared as I shall ever be. If only I felt a little stronger. This beastly ague strikes me down intermittently and casts a strange light on what happened over there. I feel as if I've stepped through the mirror to the other side: I watch those around me carrying out their daily tasks but they do them the wrong way round, as it were. I'm here and not here at the same time and feel like a savage inside, terrified in case anyone should guess how much I have changed. Oddly enough, they don't. Mother declares I'm just the same, perhaps a little thinner in the face, by which I think she means I've lost my looks. As Jane was always the pretty one I'm not too fussed about that.

You may have heard what happened at Aden. Perhaps you saw the General on your return? They weren't, I can safely say, very pleased to see me and my presence in the town caused them the acutest embarrassment. An invitation to stay at the Residency was out of the question, nor could they let me roam, so I was kept under lock and key by a merchant family near Steamer Point, a state to which I acclimatized myself with ease.

General Harris called me to an interview in Crater Town, despatching a *gharry* and his bodyguard to escort me personally. As I travelled the four bone-shaking miles, past the harbour at Ma'la crowded with dhows and native craft, up the winding road to Main Pass and down into the stinking desolation of Crater itself, I wondered at the joys I had experienced there on my previous visit, the joys of brushing shoulders with some gorgeous sheikhs, and breathing again the heady perfumes of Arabia, its peculiar blend of casual filth and myrrh. Now I saw it for what it was, a barren land baked biscuit-brown by the sun where nothing grew of its own volition and where the walls of Jebel Shamshan closed in around me like a very dreary prison. My journey had reached its end, a rather miserable end in this hideous garrison town, and I understood at last that endings are never worth the hardships one endures.

The General received me politely enough. His famous temper walked upon a leash and he went so far as to offer me a glass of Madeira, not the best. I met him, you know, as a child during his frequent visits to Maunton and remembered him as a very hale and hearty sort, the bluffest of companions. One's perspective as a small girl, riding the knees of family friends, is apt to mislead in later life.

The past is behind me now and best forgotten as quickly as possible – an express condition of my very limited rehabilitation. India has decreed that because of its conclusion no word of my journey must emerge. The whole affair has been scrubbed from the history books as if I never went to Māreb at all and, should the Turks attempt to wave my piece of paper under our noses, we're to shout 'foul' in unison and dismiss the work as a forgery. This bears out one of the elementary rules of diplomacy under which it's not the truth that counts but how snugly one wears the mantle of deceit. I gladly gave the General my word and shall stick to it, come what may, in a vain attempt to mend the tatters of my threadbare reputation.

They had me to dine once at the Residency, a rather grand affair in honour of the successful conclusion of the month-long Coronation festivities, a sort of dinner to end dinners. I was seated out of harm's way towards the bottom of the table next to a Herr Kappelhof, the German Consular Agent, a bone and guano merchant by trade. (A consul who sells bird droppings for a living: can you imagine it? I know I shall never comprehend the ways of diplomacy.) The talk was mainly of the Imam and Turkish prospects in the *vilayet*. The views expressed were frankly eccentric but you'll be pleased to know I held my tongue.

The dinner was anyway frightfully dull, apart from the opportunity it gave me to pick up the threads of my acquaintance with Captain Kincaid, who chatted pleasantly when his superiors looked the other way. He said that when the General heard the news from San'ā he called for me to be locked up in a lunatic asylum for the criminally insane. Lady Harris apparently shares his opinion. I overheard her tell another guest, Signora Spelli, wife of the Italian Consul-General, that I come from a very queer family and that my people are in trade. I haven't relayed the remark to Mother who would take greater offence than such a casual snub deserves.

But Captain Kincaid is a better sort altogether. He has a clean-jawed Army face that one knows will make him a major before he turns thirty-two. If you see him again, please send him my regards. To his immense credit, he took me one evening to the Club where we listened to the gentle lappings of the ocean and the band's military airs and I was cold-shouldered by everyone else. As you can imagine, I was glad to be rid of them and they of me.

The voyage home was equally tedious. On hearing (not from me, *pace* the General) that I knew something of the Yemen, one of the other passengers, a clerk from the Aden firm of Luke Thomas & Co., asked if I had encountered the daring Mr Fergusson, about whose exploits they were all agog. I kept to my cabin after that and had my meals sent down.

I come across his name at every turn. When passing through London, I called in on Scott Keltie at the Royal Geographical Society in Burlington Gardens. The Society had lent me some instruments, which I felt honour-bound to return. (Remember that my journey was never made.) He attributed my failure to the fact that Fergusson had got there first. 'Damned bad luck,' he said, patting my knee in consolation. 'He's giving a lecture tomorrow night. I'll get you tickets if you like. He's bound to want to meet you after this.' His kind offer I regretfully declined. Apparently the Society intends giving him their Gold Medal, an honour I hope he values as much as he should.

After London I travelled north to my family, overjoyed to be reunited with them at last, especially my dear sister Jane, the sweetest of beings, who will shortly leave us as she's to be married in the spring. Edward has already flown the nest so we shall make a very small party. At least my skills will be required: Mother is ailing and Father plagued by gouty pains. My spell in the desert has made me very good at sickbeds; and when I'm not at home I walk the dear, remembered hills, every rock and gully known to me from earliest times, and often wonder at my previous desires to travel further afield. My only quarrel with Jane is that she gave the Foreign Office a letter I'd written from Aden, for her eyes alone. She said she did it for my greater safety and so I forgave her too. It was the letter that alerted them to James, to Mr Fergusson. I'm not sure in the end it made much odds. What's done is done and who are we to try and unravel the threads?

I keep reading accounts of his Great Journey. They bother me terribly. He claims that Māreb is the site of Sheba's kingdom which is wrong, completely wrong. The dates are incompatible. King Solomon died in about 930 BC, while nothing we found at the temple predates 600 BC. She never came from Māreb at all unless she travelled back in time, and I don't hold with that sort of jiggery-pokery. She came from the north. The confusion I attribute to later historians who mistook Saba or Sheba for a place when really it refers to a people. And people move. They drift about, shifting with the sands.

Nor has the Bilqīs of Arabian lore any connection whatsoever with the biblical Queen of Sheba. Their stories merged haphazardly to become what they are today, a dangerous brew of fact and fantasy. The Arab has a very short memory though he professes to remember Methuselah.

Do you know, I've thought once or twice of writing an article for one of the learned journals to set the record straight but am restrained by my promise to the General, which would require it to be done anonymously and I'd rather not stoop to that. I comfort myself with the knowledge that later scholars will correctly interpret the evidence and throw his theories out of the window. It's not that I mind what he did to me but I do resent his wilful obfuscation of the facts.

And yet, you know, I did love him. I loved him from the moment he propositioned me in the *sūqs* of Aden where he'd sent a servant to seek me out. The chap had a hare lip and looked a very shifty type. I couldn't follow his drift. He gabbled something about his master and a hedgehog and heaven knows what besides. Then Fergusson appeared in a whiff of smoke like a true genie of the lamp and brooked no argument.

'Will you come with me, Miss Grace?' he asked, fixing me with those unwavering eyes, as black and deep as sin. 'The roads are several. We can part, if we quarrel. The spaces over there will give us both room to breathe.'

He offered to find me a passage out of Aden, claiming that with my introduction to the Turks and his to the tribesmen we were bound to succeed. Reading between the lines, I thought he wanted to hitch his carriage to my growing reputation and though the reality was more straightforward – he wanted my money, pure and simple – I'd go with him again if the opportunity arose. He offered me treasures more precious than all the stones of Arabia, more precious even than the head he stole. He offered to set me free. Not from any material fetters, you understand, but from the shackles of my own creation.

To write of this has raked the embers of my memory. He crackles and spits in my imagination, refusing to be doused. If you could only see him as I do you might understand why I would give him a second chance.

He came to see me a while back, dropping by un-announced in his inimitable fashion. Like any bad penny one never knows when to expect him next. He found me in the library where I was helping Father to catalogue his books. I couldn't run away. We entertained him to tea, Mother at her most gracious because she'd read of him in the newspapers, and mistook him for a personage when he's really the devil himself. She even requested Jane to play for him some airs on the piano, explaining (in my presence) that, though I was the elder of her daughters, Jane had taken more than her fair share of accomplishments.

He turned on me a smile of such tenderness mixed with a hint of concern that I must shut my eyes to forestall an obvious demonstration of how miserable I felt.

Strange though it may seem, the occasion passed off without incident. James knows how to win hearts when it pleases him and had clearly determined to treat my mother to the best of his charms until she all but drowned in his praise. Instead of inspiring in me a sense of disgust, his blatant falsehoods rekindled my spirits so that I joined Jane at the piano, banging the keys in very jolly abandon.

After a decent interval, James asked to be shown the grounds, having heard, he said, of their magnificence. We had to stop Mother accompanying us on our walk.

I took him to the lake, spread with a tangle of rotting water lilies so dense that one might walk across their floating leaves from one end to the other. Around us flared the final colours of autumn and we sat for a time in the summer house which smelt of mildew and the dark, dank earth. The spot was deathly still; I thought he must have heard the beating of my heart. A solitary moorhen glided through the reeds. I knew he wanted me to make it easy for him but all my sufferings rebelled and I was damned if I would let him off the hook.

And so I sat and waited, my anger mounting as I wondered what rabbits he would whip from his coat-sleeves to explain his many crimes. Not for the first time I found my judgement of him wanting because when he spoke at last he shrugged off any attempt at explanation, or excuse, saying merely that for me he'd put his head on the block. I could ruin him if I chose, he wouldn't complain.

'How do you mean, ruin you?'

'The story of my journey . . . It wasn't mine at all. One word from you and my pack of cards will collapse.'

'I can't,' I said curtly. 'I've given the General my word. You may one day be exposed as a liar but never, sir, by me.'

'You were sick, Elinor. I couldn't take you with me. The Turks were your only hope.'

'Then why did you paint me as a gun runner?'

'I needed time.'

'You bought yourself plenty of that.'

He had the audacity to smile at me. 'Are you very sore?' he asked, placing both hands on my shoulders and staring hard into my eyes. I smelt a trace of spirits on his breath. As I tried to pull myself free, his fingers brushed my neck. I felt a flush of fear; and yet I longed to throw myself into his arms and hear how he might try to comfort me. He looked at me carefully, as if he were trying to fix the lines of my face in the fluid of his memory.

'You know, Elinor,' he said, 'you misrepresented me terribly. The picture you drew of me in your journal, I'm not like that at all.'

'My journals? You took those too, on top of everything else? How *could* you?'

The thought that he was privy to my innermost wonderings made me die a little inside.

'I read them on my voyage home. Several times. And at each reading I asked myself over and over again: did I really look so black? Was I really that hard on you? You've painted me as someone I don't recognize. I wondered if you knew me at all or whether I appeared as you wished me to be. Damn it all, Elinor, we had some good times together – don't you remember? You've not touched on those.'

I don't expect I'm making much sense. I'm merely trying to explain that he was maybe not as bad as we have all assumed. In every tale there's more than one point of view.

He talked to me then of a night I would rather forget, up in the mountains, before we quarrelled over the guns. Some tribesmen came to our camp, two I remember, wildness incarnate. They came from the Imam and gave him money, lots of it, which he later lost along with everything else. A terrible night, demonic in tone. They danced for him in flames, a coven of witches cavorting on the blackest of nights. I think we all lost our heads. But what he remembers most is my face through the flames. I looked like a queen, he says, ringed with darkness and a solemn watchfulness that never broke, not once. Do you know, he was frightened of me then. He says that a terrible power came out from me on the other side of the flames and that he feared not for himself but for his dreams which I might snatch away. He could not let that happen. His dreams were much too dangerous, for both of us. That's why he started the quarrel between us, and sent me away.

This memory jolted my senses. We could have done so much. My love for him could have led us to a brighter world than the one to which we have returned.

Unable to bear the interview a moment longer, I rose hurriedly and offered to direct him to the gates. We walked side by side, my hand on his arm. I willed myself to be strong, knowing that this was the very last time we would walk together and that I must be present to the end.

We talked of this and that. Yūsuf, I'm afraid, never made it to the coast. Up in the mountains he grew very jumpy, saw spirits everywhere, in the trees, and the stones, and the odd watercourse. They chased him over a precipice beyond the walls of Menākhah and, when James had finally scrambled down to see what he could do, Yūsuf had all but met his Maker. James finished him off with a clean bullet to the brain, a kinder fate than the one he meted out to 'Ali. But I forgot, you never knew 'Ali, did you?

Now he's back in Glasgow making a sort of life for himself. He says it rains unendingly and that the smell of peat bogs makes his nose twitch. The people scuttle about with their heads down, blind to the world out there, a whole ripe world ready for the plucking.

He's back with his wife Ann, as reconciled as they will ever be. He told me about her in Māreb, a little late in the day, and his daughter Caroline. I offered to give her a home and would have learned to love her as my own. The world he promised Ann lies just around the corner. A second child is on the way. If it's a girl, he says he'll call her Elinor.

At the gates he thrust into my hand a package enclosing the money he owed and more, saying he'd not demean either of us by putting a price on everything he took. We said our brisk farewells and as I watched him disappear from view he never once looked back to wave at me. The rest of the evening I had to endure Mother's compliments on my delightful friend, whose only fault was that he had omitted the simple courtesy of bidding her goodbye.

I'll never forget him, ever. He says he'll never forget me either but, as you and I know to our cost, he's not a man for keeping to his word. He's changed me, for good or ill. He took me to a harsher world where one lives on one's wits and where we shed the baggage of our European habits until we stood alone in all that emptiness. He taught me things about myself, things I'd rather not have known, but he opened the lid and let my demons fly out. They've gone now, flown into the desert, leaving behind a chasm at my centre, clean and empty like an aching heart which I must carry with me into society and hope that no one notices the desolation within.

My hand shakes as I write this but the line is drawn, dear Doctor: I've travelled to the bottom and survived. If fate threw us together again I honestly believe I could exchange with him a civil word. And as my pain is put to bed I shall return the ledger to its shelf and submerge myself once more in the ordinary business of living.

All that remains is to ask you to remember me to Mary and send a kiss to Elizabeth. They looked after me splendidly during my convalescence and I'll think of you all, my dear, dear friend, with the greatest affection and respect. One day I hope to repay your many kindnesses, and make good the damage I have done.

With heartfelt gratitude,
Elinor

POSTSCRIPT

Elinor Grace's letter was returned unread, as Dr Wendell had already been dismissed. The stated pretext was that he had aroused resentment among the Arabs who suspected him of feathering his nest, but in reality he took the blame for what had become known to a small, select few as the Grace Affair. All reference to her journey was erased from official files, an unnecessary precaution as 'Izzet Pasha never, in the end, availed himself of her 'confession'.

In 1912, 'Izzet Pasha returned to Stamboul to seek ratification from the Imperial Parliament of his agreement with Imam Yahya. This goal was finally achieved the following year when an Imperial Firman was read publicly at San'ā to the accompaniment of much rejoicing and firing of guns, declaring an official entente with the Imam 'for the sake of peace between Moslems'. He left in charge, as Vali, Mahmūd Nazīm Bey, the previous Vali having been dismissed for his dilatory performance against the Idrīsi rebels, when he lost upwards of a thousand men.

James Fergusson was accorded the Patron's Medal of the Royal Geographical Society in 1912. He wrote a book about his travels to Māreb, entitled *Sheba's Lands*, donated the Queen's supposed head to the British Museum and was much in demand on the lecture circuit even in America where interest in the Yemen ran high. His second daughter, Louisa Elinor, was born on 15 March 1912. As part of his legacy the ruins at Māreb continue to be linked to that mysterious queen who came bearing spices and very much gold to hear the wisdom of Solomon.

After her brother and sister were married within a short space of each other, Elinor remained at Maunton, tending to the needs of her parents and taking every opportunity to walk among her dark, Northumbrian hills. Edward had a son and Jane produced twin boys whose frequent visits gave her much to do. As a favourite aunt, she became a most proficient story-teller, enchanting her nephews with exotic tales of the East. They were too young to appreciate the darker edge to her stories, or to recognize the prickly tang of saltpetre that lingered in the air. Among her many domestic activities, she compiled a photographic record of her extended family and wrote plays to be performed at Christmas with a small part for everyone. She never travelled again.

ELINOR GRACE'S JOURNEY TO MĀREB IN SOUTH-WEST ARABIA

A NOTE ON THE AUTHOR

Jennifer Potter lives in London where she works as a corporate copywriter. As well as an earlier novel set in Martinique, *The Taking of Agnès*, she wrote the original story for Christopher Petit's film, *Flight to Berlin*, shown in the cinema and on Channel Four. She has one son.